T0156649

A Special Assignment

A novel about spiritual warfare

DOUG TANNER

Order this book online at www.trafford.com
or email orders@trafford.com

Most Trafford titles are also available at major online book retailers.

Print information available on the last page.

ISBN: 978-1-4907-9212-5 (sc)
ISBN: 978-1-4907-9214-9 (e)

Trafford rev. 11/13/2018

www.trafford.com
North America & international
toll-free: 1 888 232 4444 (USA & Canada)
fax: 812 355 4082

ACKNOWLEDGEMENT

This is my first book and it has been a challenge. I would like to thank my wife, Patti, for believing in my abilities and for encouraging me to try. She said she always thought I should write a book and it is because of her belief in me that I attempted this. I want to thank my daughter Brindy for editing this work and helping me with my grammar and sentence structure and for my Son in Law, Jeff, who has been so good to her and has been an encouragement to me in the way he has overcome obstacles in his life. Thank you to my Son and Daughter in Law, Jason and Lauren, for being such an inspiration in the way they have sacrificed so much for our country. Thank you to my daughter Leah who is such a great Mom and daughter and to my Son in Law, Micheal, who has shown me what hard work and perseverance can accomplish. I want to thank all my children for making me so proud to be their Dad. All the main characters in this book are named after my children and grandchildren so that maybe one day, when I am gone, they will read this and know that I loved them and thought about them all the time. My greatest thank you goes to my Lord and Savior Jesus Christ who gave His life for me so that I can be forgiven of my sins and one day make Heaven my home.

CONTENTS

INTRODUCTION

The world we live in is made up of two realms and we fail to see one which makes the other difficult to understand. I am speaking of the physical and the spiritual realms. As humans we have a hard time understanding why things happen, especially when bad things happen to good people. Our reasoning is often one-sided and is limited to our experiences or the experiences of others. Behind the scenes there is a warfare going on that is shaping our present and future. What we fail to see and to understand is the fact that we are spiritual creatures and we simply live out our physical existence in order to fulfill our spiritual purpose. This battle is between good and evil and the objective is the souls of men, women, boys and girls. I am convinced that if we could see and understand this supernatural spiritual war-fare going on around us we would change the way we live our lives and our priorities would change. The Bible teaches us that we wrestle not against flesh and blood but against spiritual wickedness in high places. We wrestle against principalities and powers of the air. To put it plainly, we wrestle against demons and the powers of hell that are trying to stop God's plan of redemption. The Bible also teaches that each person has an angel assigned to them to protect them. This book will take a look into that other realm and try to encourage you to look beyond your circumstances and troubles to see the big picture. Everything happens for a reason and everything has a purpose. As a believer in Jesus Christ, you are an enemy of Satan and Hell. Their one purpose is to stop God. Satan wanted to be God and since he can't, he will attack the very object of God's Love: you!

CHAPTER ONE

THE BEGINNING

"Why are we waiting in line?" he asked, as they inched slowly toward the bright light. The one in front didn't say anything. He looked back at him and just gave a stare that said, 'I can't believe you don't know'. The line inches forward and he can hear faint whispers, but one voice stands out above all the rest. It is a gently soothing voice, one he has heard many times before, just never this intense. He has no memory of the past since the past is mixed in with the present and the future. Time means nothing in this place since time cannot constrain him or the others. He has only known obedience for his entire existence and has been content with it. He lives only to serve the One on the throne and finds such satisfaction in knowing his service is pleasing to his Master.

Kurios is my name and I am one of the many legions created before time and my existence is entirely for the service of the Lord of Glory. On this day I am getting the assignment to watch over this heir of salvation. I step up to the throne and stand before the shekinah glory of God. He gestures to the recording angel for a name and he returns with the name of Dustin. This is the name that was written before the beginning of time and the purpose and plan of God will find fulfillment in this human. The Father looks at his Son and you can see the amazing love between them. The Son reminds the Father that this is one for who He died and He prays for Dustin even before he is sent into the world. The Father carefully chooses the vessels who will bring Dustin into this world and will be used to care for him until the day God calls him to faith in Jesus. I can't really see the plans or the purpose, but it is not my place to know. I just obey and surrender myself to care for this heir of salvation. I am given my assignment and leave the throne of God wondering what it must be like to be loved by the Father and Son so much that they would invest so many resources. I am a created being and cannot feel emotions, but I can see what real love looks like and it must be an amazing feeling to be loved so much. I step aside and find my place awaiting the day my charge will be given the breath of life and become a living soul.

Decades turn into centuries. One soul after another is sent to the earth to be given to humans, known only as parents. God's design is for these parents to love the child and give it everything it needs to know God and choose to love God. Oh how the Father loves to see children learn about him and eventually know him as their Savior. The day finally arrives. I have watched generations pass preparing for this special time. But something seems to be wrong. I have been watching this mother and father and there seems to be love. I investigate further and see Trajor stalking them day and night, especially the one they call dad. Trajor is a crafty demon of doubt and temptation. He has been so successful in the past at getting humans to reject the love of God and if something isn't done it will happen again. I walk up behind him and say, "What are you doing here? Is there something so special with these humans that you have been sent?" He takes a deep fowl breath and slowly turns around to face me. He is a powerful demon with centuries of experience and success. His eyes glow a greenish yellow and his skin is cold to the touch. He just stares at me for a few moments then speaks. "So what are you going to be able to do? You do know that you are no match for me." He is taller than I am and he has such an intimidating presence. I start to shrink back, but then I remember my creator and the power he invested in me. I stand tall and face him and tell him he has no chance of a victory in this battle. He turns and looks toward John who is to be the grandfather of Dustin and smiles a wicked smile. He lets out a shrill laugh that stirs the slumbering demons also awaiting their chance to deceive. "So, Kurios, you think this God you serve really cares about this insignificant human about the be introduced into the world? Do you really think this male child will be any different than the others? I can assign Congerti to attack him and he will fall. Even the pitiful and weak Congerti can destroy the faith of this human family and then God's plan and purpose will be lost on another human." I walk right up to his face and stare into those yellow eyes and say "I do not fear you or your power. Even your power is given by Father God and one day you will pay for your lack of obedience." I walk away in silence and all I can do is trust Jesus that knows of Satan's plan.

CHAPTER TWO

PREPARING A WARRIOR

Perhaps we should go back in time where Dustin began in the heart of God. The Father's eyes sparkled when He spoke of Dustin. He has so many plans for this child and so many opportunities if he can find his way and keep the faith. His family was removed from their home during a very trying time and with that removal hope diminished. His grandmother, Pearl Mae, almost died when she was giving birth to Dustin's father Jackson. His guardian angel, Surmano, was busy trying to keep him alive because the Evil One saw something in Pearl Mae's life that caused him great concern. The Evil One called for Trajor and said, "I want you to stay near Jackson and do everything you can to interfere with his life, even stop his life if necessary." Trajor didn't understand but never questioned him. "Do I need any others?" he asked and was told he should be able to take care of it, but to watch out for Surmano, because he has been assigned by the Lord for some reason. Trajor laughed at the prospect of being challenged by Surmano, but he would be cautious just in case.

Pearl Mae dedicated herself to God and His work in spite of a small, annoying no-name demon of discouragement. Every time she would get a foot hold, discouragement would show up and try to cloud her mind; even to the point of intercepting her prayers. Late one night, she was agonizing before the Lord, — "why have you forsaken me? I feel so alone and I am worried about my son Jackson. Don't you love me?" Behind the curtain, where Pearl Mae could not see, Surmano was in a conflict with the demon of agony and doubt. Surmano raises his sword and blocks the attacks, but doubt keeps getting a foot hold. Surmano makes one more blow and doubt begins to run and with him agony starts to shirk back into the shadows. Surmano hopes she will keep praying and not give in. At that moment, a messenger from the throne breaks into the open holding a golden vial filled with the sweet aroma of grace. Surmano, asks, "What is your name and what is your assignment?" The angel slows and hovers for a moment. The brilliance of the residual glory from spending time in the presence of the Father is still on his face and raiment. "I have been sent with a message for Pearl Mae to encourage her in the Lord." He stops over the place where she is kneeling on calloused knees. He watches as her tears hit the floor and thinks to himself how great a faith she has. He tips the golden vial and pours it all out on her. Slowly the grace and love, straight from the Father pours into her soul. Her heart is strengthened and her face lights. She looks up staring past this messenger and utters praises, "Oh Lord, I know you love me and I know you care. Thank you precious Lord for hearing my prayers. Protect my child and increase my faith to always trust You." As these prayers come from her heart, Trajor attempts to swoop down and cause grief, but Surmano ducks in quickly to intercept. Doubt and Fear also attempt to stop the message, but the messenger already has the power of her faith and He quickly darts past these demons straight to the throne of God. He is not surprised at the power of prayer and praise, and thanks God that he has been assigned to carry this message of faith. If only all humans would hold on like her.

Pearl Mae reaches up and grabs the side of the bed and slowly pulls herself to her feet. Her knees hurt and her heart is breaking, but her mind is determined to stay faithful. She takes a deep breath, stretches and looks straight up toward the water-stained ceiling of her small humble home. She stops and holds her breath as if she sees something. She is motionless as she continues to stare. Surmano hovers over her and protects her from any outside influence. She whispers a prayer of thanks and a smile slowly forms on her weathered face. Her crooked teeth show the years of going without proper dental care not because she didn't care, but because she was responsible for everything. Her husband, John, was taken from her in a terrible accident and now she faces the unknown of raising a child alone. She starts singing a little song that her mother taught her, "I am not alone, I belong to you. Keep me safely in your arms just like you promised to." She smiles again and finds a renewed strength as she makes her way to the kitchen. She reaches in her bare cupboard for a little sugar and flour. Morning will be here before she knows it and Jackson will be hungry. She mixes the ingredients as she sings her little tune. Her heart is alive in spite of the worry that permeates her mind. She places the dough in a pan to rise and places it on the stove. She makes her way back to her bed and lays down. Her mind thinks about all she has in spite of all she does not have and she slowly drifts to sleep. The Holy Spirt now fills her mind with grace and peace. Surmano takes his place above her bed and stands guard for this saint as he anticipates what tomorrow will hold.

Years have passed since that prayer time. Daily she would pray and trust, and trust and pray. Jackson is growing and each day she teaches him the Word of the Lord. She sings to him and instills in him the faith she has practiced all these years. Surmano is now joined by another powerful angel known as a mighty warrior who has won many battles against the powers of darkness. His assignment is to watch over Jackson and assist Surmano as he protects Pearl. This warrior is called Ishnea and he is determined to make sure Jackson reaches the age of accountability and that any evil influence that would want to stop the plan of God in Jackson's life will be eliminated. Jackson is now 10 years old and Pearl Mae has taught him well. He is showing a real spiritual maturity and each Sunday they take the long walk to their small insignificant church. This one a particular Sunday something is different. Surmano and Ishnea go ahead of them clearing the way and standing guard inside the sanctuary. Just prior to them arriving the old country pastor is praying that all demons and evil be kept at bay at the door and he is praying that they not be given a place in the service. As Surmano and Ishnea arrive they see Trajor and another demon approach. They intercept their path and block their entrance. A short battle ensues. Evil will not win this day, but Trajor and the other demon do not give up. They wait outside for other humans to arrive. They know from experience not everyone that is coming today will have a heart for God. They will carefully choose several of the members and influence their thoughts. A call is made for several smaller demons with special abilities to assist. One is the Spirit of Judgement. He lands next to one of the members and makes him think of all the things that is wrong in this small church. He puts it in his mind to make sure he is short with people and points out that the pastor did not visit him. He reminds the pastor he

7

pays his salary. The other demon speaks to the member who has bought a new outfit today and will make sure she flaunts it in front of those who can't afford anything. They might not be able to enter the church building because of Surmano and Ishnea, but they can influence the thoughts and attitudes of those inside, and through them they can discourage the people who are trying to change their lives. Trajor focuses on Jackson because he knows enough about God to know God has his eye on this young man and he must stop him before it gets out of hand.

The Spirit of God is here today and is touching the hearts of people. He speaks to the pastor who opens the Word of God. Heaven stops what they are doing and looks at this small congregation. The Lord is pouring out His Spirit and the praises from these few believers builds and builds. As if from a smoldering fire, the flame grows and the smoke rises to the portals of heaven. The Father and the Son watch intently and are moved by this worship. The power of God is so strong that it knocks the demons backwards and away from this gathering of believers. Even the ones influenced by judgement and pride are being touched. The hard exterior is falling away and they fight to hold on to their ungodly attitudes. The power of the preaching of the word sends out arrows of conviction. The Holy Spirit grabs at each heart and slowly surrender comes from the lips and heart of almost everyone in the service. "For by grace, His grace, are you pulled from the fiery stinging grip of hell...?" The pastor continues with a new found joy in his voice, "The Lord is not slack concerning his promises, can I get an Amen?" The congregation answers back. Ladies are standing now raising their handkerchiefs. The men raise hands in praise and affirmation. "Lift up your heads", the pastor conveys with a smile in his eyes and a strong demand in his voice. "I said lift up your heads! Give Him your life, trust him with your heart" Words of praise, "amen, amen, hallelujah", comes from the congregation. Power is now pouring in from above. The faith of Jesus is being given out and Jackson rises to his feet. He no longer fights the urge and walks down the aisle. Surmano and Ishnea hover over and are almost envious of this group of believers. How it must feel to experience the grace and power of God. How it must feel to experience this love from God. They watch as Jackson almost starts running to the old fashioned wooden altar. He kneels and in a brief moment of time seals his forever. He surrenders to the Lord and gives Jesus his life. At that moment the Father speaks to an angel seated at a beautiful white table with a large book sitting on it. The angel, with pen in hand awaits the command of God to record another name. What a joy to write another name. With the swipe of a pen he writes the name 'Jackson'. There is now, in the presence of God, rejoicing over one soul that repents. Heaven's bells ring in victory and hell trembles as another soul loosens its grip on the world. Forever is sealed and the plan of God continues through this soul. Pearl Mae watches in amazement and her heart fills with the presence of God. She raises her calloused and crippled hands toward heaven. She sways gently at the sound of Amazing Grace. She smiles and sings, "Thank you Lord, thank you Lord, thank you Lord." Heaven is smiling but the battle is just beginning.

Jackson and Pearl walk home along a winding country road. The smell of jasmine from the fence line along the road fills the air and both of them feel like they are walking on clouds. "Mama", Pearl looked over at him with smiling eyes and a great big grin and answers, "yes baby." Jackson stops and turns her toward him and says, "Mama, what do you think God is going to do with me? Do you think I can be like the pastor one day?" Pearl looked intently at him for a few seconds then put her leathery hands on both sides of his face and shook his head slightly from side to side and said, " Baby, I believe Jesus has more planned for you than that. I love our pastor and our church, but there is a big old world out there and a whole lotta people that need to hear about Jesus. Jesus has a special place for you in this world and as long as you leave it up to Him and trust Him with all your heart, He will do even more than we can dream." Jackson smiles a great big smile then gets up on his tip toes and hugs Pearl with all his might. "Mama", Jackson said, "I love you." She held him tight and said, "I love you too baby, let's get home and get some dinner." They start walking again as Surmano and Ishnea follow behind making sure they are safe.

School started and Jackson is a good student. He is hungry to learn and takes advantage of every chance to read. His favorite book, however, is the old Bible his daddy used to read to him when he was a baby, just before he died. He loves reading the notes his daddy left in the Bible and thinks the notes were meant just for him. His favorite verse and notes are in John 14:1. 'Don't let your heart be troubled, you believe in God believe also in me, in my Father's house are many mansions and I go to prepare a place for you.' The notes his daddy wrote are really good. It doesn't matter where you live here on earth, because our real house is being built in Heaven and God has a moving day planned. Believe it! Jackson closes his eyes and tries to imagine what that house will look like. Daddy already had his moving day and he is waiting for us. Surmano and Ishnea listen to Jackson talk about heaven and they want so badly to tell him how beautiful and peaceful it is. They were there when Jackson's dad came home and met Jesus. They want to tell Jackson that his daddy is safe and enjoying the presence of God, but it is forbidden to speak to humans. They are allowed to show themselves to the humans in their charge, but they can't be told they are angels. Only a select few humans have the faith to really believe that angels are active in their lives and they think Jackson will be one of them. Jackson closes his daddy's bible and gets down on his knees and says, "Jesus, thank you for building me a house where you are. I think it is going to be fun when I get there. Tell daddy I said hi and that I will take good care of mama. Thank you for saving me and for loving me and mama, in Your name I pray, Amen." The prayer angel grabs the prayer and immediately takes off. He gains speed as he approaches a group of demons standing in the path waiting to intercept him. All of a sudden a bright flash of light and that wall of opposition breaks apart like bowling pins being knocked over. As quick as he grabbed the prayer he is gone and is in the presence of the Father. The sweet aroma of this child's prayer fills the throne room and all the angels watch in awe as the Father smiles. Jesus looks over at Jackson's dad and tells him of this young, powerful saint that he helped to influence. From the day that Jackson was formed in the womb, the Father has been sending grace and mercy to prepare this child for what lay ahead. The accuser of the brethren, the one that is before God's throne to blame and accuse all men, tries to figure out God's plan for Jackson, but he can only speculate. The last time he saw God take a special interest in someone like this was when God told Boaz to take Ruth to be his wife. The wicked one knows that led to the birth of King David and all the powerful things God did through him. If he guesses correctly, this Jackson needs to be a target. Perhaps he needs to send someone to help Trajor. He calls his general and commands him to send Draden to assist Trajor with special instructions to find out what really moves Jackson and learn how to use it against him. Draden hates an assignment like this because human faith is so unpredictable and anything can happen unexpectedly. There will be no rest from this day forward. If the master sees something then they must pay close attention. Maybe if they can convince Jackson they are on his side they can cause his fall.

Pearl has a hard time dealing with the demands of a single mother. Every morning she goes through the same routine. She gets up way before daylight and heads to the kitchen. She makes her some tea and while the water is heating up she kneels down beside the old couch in the living room. The house isn't anything to look at and all the furniture is worn out. The wallpaper on the walls has been peeling for years and the roof has water stains in several locations. The living room is a small space connected to the kitchen by a small set of cabinets with plain white wooden doors and dark round metal handles. Some of the hinges are coming off the cabinets and those cabinet doors lay crooked on the cabinet. She has to lift the door to make sure it shuts tight against the frame. There is one single light hanging from the ceiling and its dim glow makes it hard to see anything. The loud whistle from the tea pot sounds and she is startled for a moment because she was so deep in her thoughts. She makes herself a cup of Chicory tea with a little sugar and makes her way to the old rickety kitchen table. She sets her cup down and opens her Bible. It is a thick book with a weathered leather cover and torn pages hanging out of the side. She opens it to Palms 37:7 and reads. Be still before the Lord and wait patiently for him. She closes her Bible then closes her eyes. She meditates on the word from the Lord. She ponders in her mind about waiting. It seems like she is always waiting on the Lord and he never seems to be in a hurry. She thought her life was over when Jackson's daddy died and it seemed like God was silent. She thinks about all the waiting she has done in her life. She waited for the pain of losing the love of her life to go away, but it never did. It just got a little easier to bear because she had Jackson. She waited for God to provide a better living for her and Jackson and each time He gives just enough to make it through. They never did without, but always had to fight envy. She begins to pray, "Father, I hope you don't get upset with me for saying this, but it is really hard to wait on you much longer. I ain't sure if you are even hearing me, but I am gonna keep believing that you got a plan bigger than my discouragement and pain." She takes a sip of her tea and enjoys its warmth on her throat. She reaches over to a small basket on the table and takes out a sweet potato biscuit and takes a bite. "Thank you Jesus for this food and this tea" she prays, "thank you for taking care of me and my boy. I love you Lord and I want to thank you for loving me more than I can imagine."

Jackson wakes up and makes his way from his small bed that is in a corner just off the edge of the living room. He shuffles to the table where his mama is singing and holding her tea cup with both hands. He sneaks up behind her and kisses her then throws his small arms around her and gives her a big hug. "Mama, I love you" he said, "hope you had a good night's sleep. Can I have the last bit of milk?" "Sure baby", she said, "I am getting more today when I get to work. I'll bring it home with me tonight" "Ok Mama!" Surmano has been keeping watch all night and has been keeping his eye on two small demons who have been sitting outside the window. He recognizes one as the spirit of distrust and the other one is the spirit of doubt. They want to get into Pearl and Jackson's mind so bad they can almost taste it. The talk to each other and make plans to get to Jackson while he is at school. They make the mistake of speaking out loud where Surmano can hear. Jackson grabs his books and what little lunch Pearl made him and he steps out of the door. Surmano steps out with him keeping an eye on doubt and distrust. They circle the pair as

Jackson walks to school. One dives in to try to get in Jackson's mind while the other one engages Surmano, but that was a mistake. Surmano grabs doubt by this neck and flings him with all his might. Doubt flees when he realizes he is no match for Surmano. Distrust almost makes it to Jackson, but just as he approached, Jackson starts singing an old hymn, "Praise him, Praise him, Jesus our blessed redeemer" Distrust can't stand that name and hates praise. He stops in midair and this distraction is just enough time for Surmano to catch him by one leg. Distrust pulls back and tries to kick free, but Surmano is too strong. One more attempt to get away is just what Surmano needed to get a better hold. He twirls him around and around then releases him. Both distrust and doubt are sent away and Jackson continues on his way not realizing the warfare that just took place.

CHAPTER THREE

THE FIRST TEST

As it always does, time marches on and Jackson grows in faith and knowledge. Pearl has given him every opportunity and Jackson has taken advantage of it. He is now in High School and is a handsome young man with multiple talents. Everything he attempts to do it done with excellence and ease. His faith has grown, but so have the questions. He has been protected all of his childhood. The powerful prayers of Pearl have been effective. There were times reinforcements had to be sent in because it was obvious to the wicked one that this young man was special to God and God's hand was on him. What the wicked one failed has always failed to realize is that the Father has his hand on all his children, it is just that all of His children do not have their hand on God. Jackson is one of those who has their hand on God. Jackson makes faith look so easy. Every time something comes up he always had a word from the Lord and this, combined with the prayers of Pearl, has kept his eye on the prize. However, something is starting to happen to Jackson that Surmano can't understand. Jackson is starting to ask questions that go against the things he has been taught and it appears someone has gotten through when Surmano wasn't paying attention, but when was that? An angel never sleeps and never tires. There are a lot of demons that come and go. Some seem to be powerful and some insignificant. Is it possible one of them slipped through and started getting into Jackson's mind?

Jackson is 16 years old and has met a young lady at school that has caught his eye. Two special demons have been sent to work behind the scenes and they are using an old tactic to get Jackson distracted. They were there when God created Eve and saw the look on Adams face when God gave her to him. They know that God placed a strong physical desire in men for women and they want to be able to use it against Jackson, maybe this is the weakness they were looking for. Pearl doesn't know about this young lady, but she knows something is different about Jackson. His time studying Gods word has been less and he seems to be praying less. He gets ready for school quickly and is out of the house anxious to get to school. There has been numerous occasions that he has come home late and barely spoken to her when he does get home. Jackson comes home and when he comes in the door Pearl meets him at the door, "hey baby" she says, and "how was your day?" He drops his books on the old table and without stopping says, "it was ok" then goes to his bed and lays down. Pearl follows him and walks up to him and taps him on the shoulder and smiles. "Can we talk" she asks. He responds by asking what she wants to talk about and she says, "I just want to spend a little time with you and find out where you are in your walk with the Lord." He turns over and without getting up he says, "Mama, I'm okay, I just have a lot going on. I have a lot of school work and sometimes I feel like I am missing out of some fun." "What kind of fun?" she asks. Jackson looks at her with a raised eyebrow and says, "Just fun. It looks like the kids at school don't have any rules to live by and I have a lot of rules. It's not that I don't love the Lord and trust Him, but it seems like all He wants us to do is keep a bunch of rules and it seems like His rules are always against fun." Pearl thought this day might come and has been preparing for it. She utters a little prayer under her breath asking for wisdom to give Jackson the right guidance. She speaks in a low soft loving voice, "Jackson, honey, I know there are a lot of things tugging at your heart and mind. I know the devil offers a lot of things that look like fun, but the fun disappears and you are left with a broken heart or regrets. Is there something special going on that you would like to talk about?" Jackson loves his mama, but he is not sure she will understand or approve, but he knows she has never given him bad advice or let him down so he decides to share. "Mama, I met a girl at school and I really like her. We talk a lot and she seems to like me to. When I am around her I feel really strange and lately she is all I think about."

News gets back to the Wicked One and he is pleased. The spirit of lust is always an effective tactic. He knows all he has to do it get a human feeling good about something and he can get them distracted from the mission God has given and this is no different. The spirit of lust is a sly one. He uses the natural attraction God placed between a man and a woman to get them to focus on things like beauty and pleasure. At first he is sure to make it innocent and casual, but through persuasion and influence he can turn the attraction into sin. The old dragon summons for the spirit of lust. Within moments a beautiful and well-spoken demon approaches accompanied by another larger less attractive demon. "Report" demands the Lord of Hell. This Jackson is a strong one and has been taught well by a dedicated and strong believer" He said.

"From the time he was in the womb she has been reading the Word of God and talking about Jesus." The big bulky demon next to him shudders at that name and lets out a foul stench as he exhales a sulfurous yellow cloud. "I hate that name" he said with disgust. "That name has been used so many times to counter act all my intentions and efforts." This big bulky demon is the spirit of greed and selfishness. He is the one who can convince a person that they deserve more than they are getting. He was the one in the Garden of Eden, when the master was deceiving Eve, telling her the advantages of eating the forbidden fruit. He was the one that convinced David to stay home from war and look at Bathsheba. When he is working with lust, they can usually cause a downfall. Satan looks at him with a stern look and asks, "So what is your plan for this young man?" This spirit of greed explains his plans. "I have been working on his mother, Pearl, to convince her Jesus must not love her. I have been showing her the life of the people she works for and convincing her that God is holding out on her. I show her all the nice things the world offers and I tell her it can be hers if she will just give up this life of faith." The evil one smiles when he remembers using that same tactic on Jesus, tempting him with all the things in the world. He really thought he could convince Jesus to worship him, but as usual, he is no match for the Son of God. "So, how is it going with Pearl", he asks. "She seems to be thinking and her prayers seem to be affected. I am planning on getting the spirit of deceit to present some gifts disguised as blessings to make her think these gifts come from God, but we have strings attached. Our plan is to get her to start enjoying some of these gifts and create a desire in her for more. We are just being delayed by a strong angel, Surmano." Satan stops for a moment then stands to his feet. He is taller than the rest and has broad, square shoulders. He is a magnificent creation with a lot of experience and knowledge. He remembers Surmano and knows he is no easy adversary. He tried to convince him to join him in the rebellion against God, but he would not leave the Father, Son and Holy Spirit. Satan asks, "Who is assigned with Surmano?" They immediately stirred and began muttering something. "With a loud voice as strong as thunder Satan said, "Enough. It seems you do not care for this helper. Who is it?" Lust said, "It is Ishnea." "With a serious and stern look on his face, Satan replies, "He is no helper, he is a powerful and strong angel that is sent to reinforce anyone with a special assignment."

He is specially chosen by Micheal when there is a potential battle ahead and he has never lost a battle. Who do we have in reserves to assist?" At that moment another demon steps out of the shadows. He is almost as big as the lord of darkness and his presence is intimidating and fearful. His big dark body is covered with scales and scars. He is the general of this Army of hell and has battle scars to prove it. He hates Micheal and Gabriel. He wants nothing more than to destroy them before they place the chains on all of them and banishes them to the lake of fire forever. His name is Strago.

Jackson met Cindy and she has changed all of his priorities. Cindy comes from a good family, but they are not Christians. They are a close family and seem to be morally good people, but they worship a different God than Jackson serves. They live in a nice neighborhood and are friends with influential people. Jackson is not sure he will fit in, but he really likes Cindy and she likes him. She knows very little about him and is anxious for him to meet her family. They hang out around each other at school every day and even arranged it so they can have classes together. There is, however, a battle going on in Jackson's mind and it is making him miserable. Surmano is doing his best to intercept the thoughts that are constantly attacking Jackson, but there seems to be reinforcements sent to attack this young man. Ishnea swoops in and stops next to Surmano and says, "We really need to be on guard and try to influence Jackson's prayer life. I saw something today I did not expect to see. I saw Strago watching at a distance." "Who, what. Did you say Strago? What could he possibly be doing here?" Ishnea remembers a time centuries ago when Strago got involved and that was the beginning of the Dark Ages. He is crafty, powerful and a master tactician. If he is here then something is happening that we need to be on our guard. Surmano asks, "Did you see any demons hanging around him?" I saw the spirit of lust and greed and another one that I couldn't identify because he went by so fast." Ishnea went on to say, "He was colorful and had a voice that was soothing and captivating." Surmano said, "Don't you remember who that is? He is the spirit of seduction. He is the same one sent to Herod's daughter to dance before Herod and then asked for the head of John the Baptist." This brought a flood of thoughts to both of their minds and they knew this was serious. There would be no rest and they must do everything they can to open the way for the Holy Spirit to work unhindered in this young man's life.

Jackson and Cindy are inseparable and they are looking for more and more opportunities to be alone. Lust is constantly hanging around and as quickly as he comes in he is gone. Just a few thoughts thrown into Jackson's mind and then he is gone. There was a time when Jackson would resist the evil and it would flee, but he is becoming lax in his prayer life and this is opening the door for something to happen. Cindy has a car, but Jackson doesn't so he keeps putting off letting her know who is really is and how poor he is. The spirit of pride follows last in each time he attacks and makes Jackson ashamed of who he is. Jackson doesn't want to tell her the truth so he makes up a story that his car was wrecked and is in the shop. He told her he is spending a little more than he wanted, but it is a classic and he wants to make sure it is done right. The Holy Spirit is grieved when Jackson makes up these stories and he moves in his heart causing Jackson to hesitate for a moment before he continues. Jackson convinces himself that the lies are not bad and he also tells himself God will forgive and understand. These are lies from the enemy and they are beginning to take their toll.

Micheal calls for Surmano and Ishnea to report to the throne room. He sends several of his personal warriors to watch over Pearl and Jackson while they are away. "Report" Micheal says. "Tell me what is happening and who is involved?" Ishnea has been in multiple battles under Micheal's command and is comfortable speaking. "There seems to be an intense focus on Jackson and we believe attacks are imminent on Pearl. Can you tell us why Hell is so concerned about this young man?" Micheal only knows what the Father and Son will reveal to him. He has never questioned them or tried to get more information from them unless they volunteer to give it. It is easy to trust the Trinity because they have never failed. They specialize in last minute deliveries, but they are only last minute because no one knows what is next. This is one of the things that really frustrates the demons of hell. They can only speculate and they never think like God. Their leader is full of pride and is power hungry and because of this he is makes a lot of mistakes. Micheal continues, "What are we doing to counteract lust and pride?" Surmano immediately answer with a confidence that borders arrogance. "We are stressing prayer and trust." How are you doing that, Micheal asks. We are trying to surround him with godly young people through a Christian sports club. It appears to be working."

Micheal looks them both in the eye and says, "all I know is that the Father has given Jackson some very special gifts and is expecting great things out of him. Surmano Jackson is just a piece of the puzzle.' Michael turns slightly and yells, "Kurios. Come here!" A quick agile angel with a sparkling smile and charismatic personality is immediately by his side jumping up and down and from side to side. "Kurios, this is Surmano and Ishnea. They will be a part of your future assignment. It is not the right time to reveal that to you, but the time is near and you must be ready." Surmano and Ishnea look at each other and smile. "Now," Micheal says, "both of you get back to your assignment and keep me informed. I will be watching and will make sure I let Strago know I am watching" As fast as they arrived they are gone. They arrive back in the lives of Pearl and Jackson and settle in for the battles ahead.

It is Sunday and it is time to go to church again. Jackson is up late and is not really interested in going this morning. Pearl nudges him to wake up and he just pulls the blanket over his head and turns over. The spirt of slumber is not a flashy demon and has never been considered a threat so he is usually ignored. This morning this spirt is working hard to stop Jackson from going to church. Strago called the demons assigned to Jackson and told them to make sure they are vigilant on this particular Sunday. The old country pastor has been interceding for his people this week and the Spirit is strong with him. He has spent time with the Lord this week and The Lord has given him a word for his people. Doubt spent some time around the pastor and heard him praying. "Lord, I thank you and praise You for calling me and trusting me with Your people. I pray You will give me unction from Your throne and make Your Word come alive with Your people." Doubt said he heard the pastor pray specifically for Jackson and the Holy Spirt really became powerful when he asked that. Surmano and Ishnea watch as Pearl wakes Jackson up and gets him to the table. Jackson fills his plate with some fresh homemade cat-head biscuits and some cane syrup. He pours a glass of cold milk and starts to take a bite. Pearl puts her hand up and says, "Baby, you need to wait just a minute. We need to thank the Lord for this food and ask Him to continue to bless us." Jackson puts the spoon down, not because he really wants to pray, but because he loves his mama. They bow their head and Pearl begins to pray, "Jesus, I am so thankful for everything you have given us. Thank you for my precious son, Jackson, and for the future you have planned for him. Bless this food so it can nourish our bodies and give us strength to serve You. We pray this in your name, amen..." Jackson looks up, still half asleep and says a weak amen then devours the breakfast.

Surmano and Ishnea go outside and begin preparing for the trip to church. They see a few demons swirling around in the distance. Nothing really to be concerned about and there is no sign of Trajor or Strago, but that doesn't mean they won't be making an appearance. The pastor opens the little church and turns on all the lights. He goes down the aisle and stops at each pew praying for the people that will be in them. In the rafters are the demons of doubt and confusion. They make sly comments and try to get into the head of this man of God, but his faith is much too strong. He stops at the back door and opens it. He looks toward heaven and smiles, he turns back toward the altar and says, "In the name of Jesus, I rebuke every evil spirit. I denounce doubt and I plead the blood against any confusion that might try to get in here today. The power of that prayer causes confusion and doubt to tumble from their perch. They are forced to leave, so they quickly exit the sanctuary, but wait outside for people to arrive. They have some favorites that come almost every Sunday and they do not come for the right reasons, so today they will be used to hinder the services.

One by one the people arrive. The pastor greets them with a smile and silently prays for each one. As they enter, the Spirit fills most of them and encourages them in the Lord. They greet each other in brotherly love and this has created a barrier that will be hard to penetrate. Surmano and Ishnea stand guard and watch in amazement and envy as the spirit fills and touches his children. The music begins and the praises of His people rise to the throne of God. Heaven is filled with the praises of this small congregation and the Holy Spirit is free to work in and through these people. Demons outside hear the praises and hate the sound. They know it will create problems as it always does and diminish their power. Trajor commands them to get closer and attempt to get inside, but they shrink back in fear. "You are cowards" Trajor screams, "They are mere mortals and have weaknesses. Find those weaknesses and exploit them." A timid demon of anxiety darts toward the open window, but is met with a loud strong wave of praise and worship. Each time anxiety tries to get into the mind of a saint, praise and worship causes anxiety to flee. The Holy Spirt whispers to the saint being targeted, "be careful for nothing, but in everything give thanks," Anxiety hates that verse because it directly targets him. He knows if he can get people to become anxious they will start to doubt God and depend on themselves and that is the best tool he has. But it is not working today.

The pastor gets up with a new spring in his step and joy in his heart. "Open the Word of God to 1 Peter." He opens his big black bible and begins to recite it from his heart, "Be sober, be vigilant because our adversary the devil is a roaring lion seeking who he may devour" he closes his bible and puts in on the pulpit. He gets a big smile, stands on his tip toes and slaps his hands together and said, "Don't you be afraid of that ole devil. He ain't no match for your Lord, He might roar, but he is toothless. Hallelujah. He tried to take a bite out of God's Son, but Jesus went to the cross and he pulled every old tooth out of that lion. We don't need to be afraid of him because greater is he that is in me than he that is in the world." Trajor hates the way they brag on Jesus. He hates the way they stand so confident behind that cross, but he knows that is where the power is. There is power in the Blood of Jesus. He watches as the faith of the saints increases and he watches Jackson lean forward and open his heart. Something has to be done. Word spreads quickly and Strago calls for reinforcements. They have to stop Jackson from committing. They need to distract him. A large swarm of dark, ruthless demons surround the church. Attack the infrastructure. Create a diversion. They must break the strong presence of the Lord. A demon causes a young person to start showing off for his friends and he loses control of his car. Going 60 miles per hour, the car veers off the road and strikes a power line. The transformer blows and the lights go out with a loud pop. The pastor stops in mid-sentence and the congregation turns to look out of the windows. Jackson stops and looks out the window too. The humans try to get back on track. The pastor calls them all to prayer and then calls for a song of praise. The deed is done and the congregation slowly falls back into the routine of church. This worship service is over and Jackson is now vulnerable again. Not Jackson only, but the generations that will follow.

Pearl and Jackson start walking home without saying a word. Pearl wants to ask him about his time at the altar, but Jackson seems a million miles away. They are almost home when Jackson breaks the silence. "Mama" he asks, Why do some people have a lot in this life and some people don't know matter how hard they work?" Pearl thinks for a minute. She wants to give the right answer, but she has often wondered that herself. Why do those who seem to try and live a Christian life, always seem to have so much less than the people who don't really care about God? Surmano hovers over Pearl so the Holy Spirit can deal with her heart and bring scripture to her mind. Pearl looks at Jackson and says, "Baby, I don't have an answer for that, but it seems like God has plans that are bigger than any one person. Why are you asking that question?" Jackson so badly wants to tell her about Cindy and her family. He has seen the great life they have and it doesn't look like they have any rules at all. He stops and picks up an old stick and starts hitting it against a big majestic oak tree just outside their door. Jackson then takes a deep breath and says," Mama, I want to introduce you to my friend Cindy and her family. They want us to come to their house today after church and I accepted for us. Would you go put on your finest dress and good shoes?" Pearl is excited to meet one of Jackson's friends even if it is a girl. Pearl goes inside and changes while Jackson gets ready to make the short trip to the other side of town. He hopes this will lead to a new life.

Pearl comes out with her favorite dress. It is a long blue cotton gown with white daisies near the hip and mid-section. She loves the smell of the jasmine perfume she picked up for almost nothing. Jackson is a little ashamed of his mom because the dress she is wearing is the one she wants to be buried in. For Pearl, just being invited by Jackson to meet the girl he is always talking to and about is exciting. Cindy's parents are at home getting everything ready for the visit that is about to take place. In preparation for this meeting, Trajor has sent envy and jealousy as well as self -pity ahead so they can plan the attack on Pearl. All three demons know their assignment and they are ready to do as much damage as possible. Word gets back to Surmano and he is also making preparations. There is a small angel that is often ignored by most demons because he is really nothing to look at, but his abilities are unmatched. He is the spirit of a sound mind and he is used by the Holy Spirit to keep saints grounded in their thinking. Pearl is going to be surrounded by a lot of things she never even dreamed of and with the demons of envy, jealousy and self-pity bearing down on her, she will need all the encouraging she can get. Pearl looks at Jackson and lifts her dress on the sides, lifts it slightly and twirls around giggling like a little school girl, "Baby" she said with a great big smile "how does your mama look?" Jackson tries to hide his embarrassment when he says, "Mama, you are more beautiful than the roses out back." She rushes over and gives him a great big hug and kisses him on each side of his face. "Don't worry honey, I am not going to embarrass you tonight. I am going to make you proud. I have been praying all week about this time and I have asked God to give you and me favor in the eyes of this family." Jackson hears a car outside and then a horn. He looks through the tattered curtains and sees Cindy waving from her car. Jackson fooled her about the car being in the shop, but how can he explain this house? They both go outside and Pearl beats him to the car. "Hey sweetie" she says to Cindy, "we are really looking forward to this and I have been praying real hard for it to go good." Cindy smiles, "I don't know what to say" she smiles then says, "Well we are so glad to have you over for dinner and cocktails tonight." "Cocktails" Pearl said, "I don't drink cocktails unless it has very little alcohol. I don't think Jesus would like to see me drinking." Pearl continues, "Cindy, honey, how do you feel about Jackson?" Cindy was taken back by the moment of boldness, but answers with a quick and limited explanation. "He is very nice and we enjoy each other's company." Then she starts the car and they drive without saying another word. Cindy looks in the rear view mirror and sees Pearl looking away. She then looks over at Jackson and mouths the words, "what was that about." Jackson just rolls his eyes and shrugs his shoulders.

On the other side of town another meeting is taking place that will possibly change the course of history for this family and many other families. Taylor Rae and Skylar Baxter are sitting in their kitchen about to eat a modest dinner. They bow their head to pray and Skylar offers up a prayer that moves the angels, Korsta and Reama. These are the angels assigned to them as heirs of salvation. They have been told that the Father has special plans for them and has arranged special protection in case Raphael interferes. Skylar prays, "Father, thank you so much for our home and for the food you have given us today. I pray for my mother that you will continue to touch her body and grant her healing from this horrible disease." Her mother, Taylor Rae, squeezes her hand then smiles at her as they place the napkins in their laps and begin eating in silence. Taylor asks how school is going and Skylar just shrugs her shoulders and said, "It is going fine, but I have a new lab partner and he is so full of himself." Taylor puts her fork down and folds her hands then asks, "Is it Jackson?" "Yes," Skylar said, "how do you know his name?" Taylor smiles and said, "I know his mother, Pearl, and we have talked about both of you." "What? Are you trying to set me up?" Taylor laughs, "No sweetheart, we are just sharing about our kids. She never suggested that and I didn't offer. I don't even know him, except for what I have seen at church, but he does seem like a nice boy." Skylar rolls her eyes, "Mom", I have no interest in him and he is definitely not my type, besides, he is a fake believer." Taylor knows she has taken this conversation a little far, so she changes the subject. "Skylar, have you decided which college you are going to attend?" Skylar responds, "Not yet, but I am leaning toward that small Christian College in North Carolina. I am not sure what God has in store for me, but I know I want to do something in missions." Korsta and Reama smile at Skylar's heart and their countenance shines as they admire this young saint. In the distance a dark figure watches. He is disfigured and grotesque to look at, but his expertise makes him one of the favorites of the Lord of Darkness. Other demons don't see what is so special about distraction, but they know he is usually called in to make sure anyone who has godly plans for their life are given options. The last time they saw distraction really attack was when the Father was trying to get America to protect innocent lives and not kill unborn babies. He worked overtime to make sure the focus was on rights of adults and not on the unborn. He was able to get the real issue overlooked and an entire nation started to look the other way. Why would distraction be here for an insignificant girl in a small town? Korsta and Reama see Distraction watching and immediately approach him, but just as they do, he takes off leaving a trail of yellow sulphuric gases behind. They know his tactics and his history, but they do not know why he is here. These are details the Father does not share.

Cindy pulls in to her driveway and Pearl is speechless. She has never seen any place like this. The gate opened without anyone getting out and the driveway is lined with beautiful giant oak trees with beautiful white, blue and green lights shining up into the trees. The front of the house is lined with giant while columns and the windows cover the entire front of the house. She has never seen windows this big and the doors are 15 feet tall and painted a beautiful shiny blue with gold inlay. They walk up 5 steps to the front door and Cindy walks in. They are met by a person wearing what looks like a like a tuxedo. Cindy Said, "Hello, Thomas" as she hands him her coat and keys. Pearl says hello and tries to shake his hand. Thomas looks at Cindy who gives him a short nod of permission, Thomas extends his hand and answers with a soft, "hello ma'am." He turns and walks away as they make their way through the giant living room to another giant room with a long wooden table with multiple chairs. The table is set with the prettiest dishes Pearl has ever seen. Another person is walking in and out of the room carrying large covered silver platters. Pearl is looking all around and is not paying attention as Cindy's mother and father enter the room. Cindy introduces Jackson and then Pearl. She smiles and with excitement in her voice says, "This is a beautiful house. Thank you for inviting us tonight." Cindy's father, Clive Roberts, extends his hand to Jackson while looking at Pearl and says, "Thank you for coming, it is our pleasure. Please won't you be seated?" They make small talk as the dinner is served. Envy, jealousy and self-pity are now in the corners of the room. They are really starting to oppress Pearl. She thinks how much she might be missing and how nice it would be for Jackson to have a future like this. She utters under her breathe how it seems so unfair that she has been given the life she has been given. At that moment, sound mind enters the room and swoops down to stand between Pearl and the three demons. They hiss and back up. This small angel clears the way for the Word of God to be free to influence her now troubled mind. Pearl stops and thinks about how much God has done for her and Jackson and is a little embarrassed by her lack of thankfulness. She looks over at Jackson and can see he is fitting in just fine. She almost feels like an outsider as Jackson and this family become engaged in conversation. Mr. Roberts looks at Jackson and says, "So Cindy tells me you are a talented athlete and also doing well in your studies." Jackson smiles as he looks at Cindy and said, "Yes sir, I have worked real hard to improve at baseball and well, I guess I have special gifts for learning. It seems to come natural to me." "Well", Mr. Roberts said, "Natural ability coupled with hard work is a formula for success." There is another demon that has been around lately and he has been following Jackson. Pride is one demon that does not need a lot of help. He has been dealing with believers for a very long time and was even instrumental in getting the Apostles to argue about their own abilities and value. Surmano has his hands full with this dinner meeting. He still does not see the reason the Father is so interested in this young man, but he can only obey the Lord and leave the results up to Him.

After the dinner was over, Cindy takes Jackson and Pearl back home. Pearl says goodbye and leaves Jackson and Cindy alone in the front yard. Jackson turns to Cindy and just stares at her. Their eyes meet and they grab each other's hands. Jackson's heart is beating so fast it seems like it is going to beat out of his chest. He watches her beautiful blue eyes move back and forth as she watches his every move. She moves closer to him and they continue just staring. Jackson starts to speak, but she raises her hand to his face and touches his lips with her finger. Lust now swoops in and whispers for Jackson to kiss her. He hesitates for a moment while the Holy Spirit moves in his heart. He is cautious, but he can't fight this feeling he has for Cindy. Jackson places his hands on either side of her face and pulls her closer. She rises on her tip toes and they lightly kiss. His mind is racing and his head seems to start spinning. They back up for a moment then embrace again only this time they do not stop. Jackson's thoughts cause the Holy Spirit to grieve. Surmano senses the grieving of the Holy Spirt and steps up his game. He motions for Sound Mind to move in closer and remind Jackson who he is.

Jackson says goodnight and Cindy leaves. He stares as the red tail lights slowly fade out of sight. He continues to stare without saying anything. His emotions are running rampant and he doesn't know what is happening. He seems frozen to the ground and unable to speak. He allows his mind to wander and it takes him to Cindy. He questions if he is doing the right thing and if Cindy is for him. He thinks about all the positives. The spirit of Lust reminds him of her beauty. Envy and greed swoop in and out whispering about possessions and what he deserves. So many thoughts and so many reasons to follow his heart. But a Sound Mind encircles him at a tremendously fast pace causing the thoughts placed by the demons to vanish. It is then Jackson says a small prayer, "Father God, I am confused right now. I want what you want, but this feeling is so strong. If this is not what you want from me, please show me." He then hears a screen door slam and the voice of Pearl calling, "Jackson, honey, are you still out there?" He answers, "I'll be right there." He looks once more down the road then upward as if acknowledging the presence of God. Tomorrow will be a new day and maybe the day his dreams come true.

CHAPTER FOUR

A PIVOTAL BATTLE

The alarm goes off early and Jackson rolls over in bed. He looks up at the tattered ceiling and prays, "Father, last night was so good and the temptation was so strong. I pray you will give me someone to keep me from making any mistakes." Immediately Surmano and Ishnea appear and surround this young saint. They make sure the small angel has plenty of room to work without interruption. The Holy Spirit is strong with this one. Pearl has been up for a while and has already prepared breakfast. She calls for Jackson to come eat and within minutes he appears. "Well Mama. What did you think about the dinner last night?" She smiles a great big smile and shakes her head from side to side and says, "Lord have mercy on me for thinking the way I was thinking last night. I told the Lord he has been holding out on me and my boy. The more I looked around me the more I felt like I was being attacked. Whatever it was, the feeling kept growing and I found myself wanting to make a deal with the devil to have those nice things, but on the ride home I found out I have everything I need in you." She places her leathery hands on his and shakes his arm. "I love you Jackson and I know our Lord has something very special for you. Please make sure you follow the leadership of the Holy Spirt when you are choosing a girlfriend. You should never get serious with anyone you can't marry." Jackson continues to stuff the pancakes in his mouth until he looks like a chipmunk. He takes a big gulp of cold milk, grabs his coat and lunch, kisses his mama goodbye and heads out the door. Above him is Surmano. Ishnea will hang around with Pearl. He loves to hear her pray.

Ahead of Jackson and Surmano is a group of demons waiting to intercept their path. Already at the school are the spirits of jealousy, hate and anger. They are working on Bobby, Cindy's old boyfriend. He has heard about Jackson and Cindy and he is not happy. Jackson is about a half mile from school and he starts having the feeling something is wrong. He doesn't know that Surmano is taking on 6 small demons who have been making an effort to distract Jackson. One of the demons breaks past Surmano and is able to throw a fiery dart of fear. Jackson tries to pray, but for some reason he is beginning to slow down and wonder if he made the right decision to confide in his mother. Now he is afraid something will happen to mess up his relationship with Cindy. He really thinks she is the one that he will be with the rest of his life. He will just have to buckle down and become the kind of man she wants. Surmano is able to fight off the rest and then finally able to influence Jackson to get rid of the fear. Surmano clears the way for the Holy Spirit to touch Jackson and make the fear go away. That dart is quenched by the grace and power of God. He continues walking to school and is just about to step inside the door when all of a sudden Bobby blocks his path. "So, you have been seeing Cindy? Do you really think you are good enough for her?" Jealousy slips in for a quick attack and is able to make Jackson really wonder if he is capable of fitting in. He has seen Bobby drive up in a nice car and he wears all the greatest styles. Much better than the rags Jackson wears. The spirits of hate and anger really get on Bobby's back and makes him begin getting physical with Jackson. Around Bobby are 4 of his buddies and they stand and watch Bobby taunt Jackson. As Jackson begins to walk off, Bobby walks up behind him and pushes him while calling him profane names. Jackson continues to walk and Surmano quickly takes his place between Jackson and the other obnoxious demons, hoping to stop this contact. Jackson is really getting mad. He whispers, "I can't take this. I don't deserve this." At that moment the Holy Spirit whispers, "You can do all things through me." He continues to remind Jackson of scripture he has studied, "be not overcome with evil, but overcome evil with good." Bobby taunts some more, "What's wrong are you even too poor to afford guts." His buddies laugh, but Jackson keeps walking. The spirit of hate jumps on Bobby and drives him, but something starts to happen. Pearl Mae is at work and is feeling a deep burden to pray, "Father, I don't know where Jackson is right now, but give him the grace he needs to endure this trial." At that moment the power of the Holy Spirit fills Jackson and he turns toward Bobby, walks right up to him and stares him in the eyes. Bobby braces in a fighting stance, but doesn't do anything. Jackson smiles and says, "you know Bobby, you're probably right. You have so much more to offer someone like Cindy. You have a nice home and I don't. You wear the best clothes and I don't. You even have a dad and I don't. But I do have hope and all I can do is the best I can with what I have and maybe one day I can be at your level." Jackson turns to walk away and as he does he is waiting for more taunting and maybe even to be hit from behind, but the intervention of the Lord has taken over and the demon of hate turns away because of the conviction of the Holy Spirit.

Bobby, cuts his eyes to the right and left and slowly turns to look at his buddies. He really feels bad now because of the way Jackson answered him. He does have a dad, but he doesn't have a very good relationship with him, almost to the pointe he doesn't have a dad either. The spirit of humility touches Bobby's heart and causes him to wonder about the courage Jackson showed. Only time will tell what will happen during the next confrontation.

No one knows what is getting ready to take place and it will alter the future of everyone in this small school. Surmano is watching Jackson when Ishnea approaches him with some news, "Surmano, Korsta and Reama are going to be joining you this afternoon. We really do not know what is going to take place, but it appears reinforcements from hell are gathering around the school. Trajor and Strago are hanging around so it must be something important they are planning. We have to be vigilant today because Jackson is going to be vulnerable and today will be pivotal in his life. Korsta and Reama are assigned to Skylar and she is not even a part of Jackson's life so why are they here?" Korsta speaks up, "Skylar is a special girl and the Lord has a special plan for her life. Somehow it seems to involve Jackson, but we don't know how. Skylar is really committed to her faith, but Jackson is struggling, so we are here to make sure Skylar maintains her balance and commitment." All of them are silent as they watch the demons swooping in and out through the trees and into the hallways of the school. Fear, anxiety, anger, jealousy are busy while the spirit of destruction paces back and forth watching Surmano and the others while whispering something under his breath. Surmano looks up then all around him as if he is looking for something. What could destruction possibly be doing here?

Pearl Mae is at work now and is trying to keep her mind occupied. The Lord has burdened her heart for Jackson for some unknown reason and she is in a constant state of prayer. "Father, you promised me you would protect me and my son. I ask, in Jesus name, that you put a hedge of protection around my baby and give him wisdom to make right choices today." The Lord heard that prayer of faith and sent Micheal to plan the tactics for the encounter that will take place on this day. A legion of angels arrive and surrounds the school. They are tall, strong and capable of turning the tide in any battle. They stand shoulder to shoulder with their swords drawn and at the ready in front of them. They don't say a word and remain in strict formation. There are no expressions on their face, only a bright glow typical of one who spent centuries before the throne. The tension is building as time slowly passes.

It is about 1:15 and the students are starting to change classes. There is a meeting with destiny that is only minutes away. Bobby, Cindy, Jackson, and Skylar will converge on a single point in time and life for all four will change. As they walk down the hall, all of a sudden there is a loud explosion that rocks the hallway where these four are walking. Surmano, Ishnea as well as Korsta and Reama jump to attention and the legion of angels raise their swords and click their heels. Thousands of angelic eyes pierce through the thin veil of mortality and stand ready to obey the master no matter what it might be.

The explosion sends flames along the top of the ceiling and through the halls. Smoke begins to pour through the halls. The fire alarms go off with a loud constant shrill causing the spirit of fear to leap with excitement. Jackson is knocked to his knees and the ringing in his ears causes him to look around him with confusion. The spirit of confusion leaps on his back and taunts Jackson, but Ishnea is able to grab fear by his scrawny shoulders and fling him hundreds of yards. The angelic hosts that are surrounding this heir of salvation are becoming restless. They know a battle is almost here and they dare not allow the powers of hell to stop Jackson from fulfilling his purpose. At the end of the hall is Bobby and Cindy. Bobby has a laceration to his forehead and one of his legs looks broken. Jackson gets to his feet, but begins coughing because of the dark billowing smoke. Cindy is laying next to Bobby, but she is Ok even though she is shaken and dazed. Jackson is strengthened by an unseen force and begins looking around as if he has lost something. He checks on Bobby and Cindy then helps them to their feet. Bobby is unable to walk so he puts his arm over Jackson's shoulder to get his balance. At that moment the spirit of revenge swoops in and taunts Jackson, "Don't you remember what he did to you today? He doesn't deserve your help. Let him get out himself." Korsta and Reama are watching over Skylar, but take a moment to double team revenge, causing him to lose his grip on Jackson. Then they return to Skylar to guard her body and mind. Jackson lifts Bobby up and drags him 40 feet to a safe place, then gently lays him down. By this time there are students and faculty gathering nearby, but the heavy smoke and flames are keeping them at a distance. Jackson looks down the hallway and sees feet sticking out from under some rubble. For a moment he freezes in fear, but his sense of duty is greater than his fear. He begins walking down the hallway while covering his face. He remembers to get down on his knees to avoid the heavy smoke, but the heat is getting intense. Demons now are doing everything they can to cause the fire to spread. Some demons begin to attack Skylar with doubt and confusion. Korsta and Reama step in and drive them away, but in the distance is another group of stronger more talented demons. There is something about Skylar that Hell felt the need for reinforcements. They come like a thick black blanket, and just as they arrive, the legion of angels surrounding the school advance from their post and block their entrance. Wave after wave attempts to get to these two young saints, but the mighty warriors sent to guard the perimeter prevail, Jackson continues down the hall until he comes to where Skylar is laying unconscious. Jackson picks her up in his arms and with a renewed strength he quickly travels the 50 feet to the safe place.

By this time fire rescue has made its way to the school and meets the four teens. While several assist the teens, the other firefighters advance on the fire and within an hour the flames are under control. Jackson is still walking around in a daze. Cindy and Bobby have already been taken by ambulance, so now the focus is on Jackson and Skylar. The paramedics are working on Skylar and her burns and broken bones. They quickly load her on a stretcher and wheel her to a waiting ambulance. Jackson watches as they take her to the hospital and he has a strange feeling that he should pray for her. "Father, watch over her and protect her." Korsta and Reama make their way to the place directly over the ambulance and watch carefully for any attacks. Jackson is leaning against a wall in the hallway when he hears a voice that sounds familiar, but he is not sure why. An old gray haired man slowly walks toward Jackson. His voice is deep and calming. Jackson looks intently at the old man and just assumes he is the janitor. Surmano is hovering very close know. He is very interested in what this elderly man will say. He speaks in a low deep voice and the moment he begins speaking the demons all around the school stop what they are doing and turn toward this man. Surmano knows him as the angel of encouragement. He was the one the Father sent when the Apostle Paul was asking the Father to remove the messenger of Satan that was attacking him. The old man steps in front of Jackson and just stares into his eyes. Jackson pushes himself off the wall and stands at attention. He is listening intently as this old man whispers to him, "lean not on your own understanding, but acknowledge God and he will direct your path." Jackson feels a strange sensation and for a moment closes his eyes. When he opens them the old man is gone. At that moment Jackson seems to get a burst of energy and suddenly the place he finds himself is not bothering him. He thinks of Bobby and Cindy and hopes they are ok, but for some odd reason he has a burden for Skylar.

The ambulance comes to a screeching halt under the concrete canopy behind the emergency room exit at Memorial Hospital. The doors of the ambulance fly open and the two paramedics jump out of the truck and remove the gurney carrying the broken body of a young woman. BP is 165 over 50 and her breathing is shallow. They push the gurney through the double doors and take Skylar into the operating room. Korsta and Reama are taking their place in the operating room. Korsta allows angels breath to sweep across the mind of the doctor who is preparing for surgery. The demons of anxiety and weariness darts back and forth in the corner of the room looking for an opening to attack this daughter of the King. One comes in to the room real fast in order to distract her guardians, but he didn't see Ishnea who was waiting for him to make a commitment. Once the demon passed a certain point, it was too late to reverse his actions. The demon of weariness slammed into Ishnea and when he did he lost his footing and place. With Korsta and Reama in the corner, they have forced any and all demons to flee, leaving a calm peace in the operating room.

In the waiting room are 4 families who have not met, but unknown to them, all four families will play a part in this amazing love story between the creator of the universe and these families. Pearl is the last one to get to the hospital. She walks up to the head nurse and says, "Please tell me where I can find my baby." "Who is he?" she asks, "He is about 5' 11 tall and wearing a gold shirt. She is looking around when all of a sudden she sees Jackson enter the room and he appears that he has been crying. "Honey", Pearl says, "Are you okay? Do you need anything?" He responds in a soft voice, "Mama, I don't want her to be hurt bad." Pearl grabs Jackson by the shoulders and pulls him to her. She whispers in his ear, "It's going to be alright, Jesus has her in his arms." They continue embracing as the busyness of the hospital continues around them. In the other world, all around are a legions of angels guarding the hospital. Just outside is a big angel with broad shoulders and clothes shining almost as if the cloth was dipped in pure gold. In his hand is a shimmering sword and he is surrounded by ten to twelve smaller angels. He summons for one to stand before him. Something is said and as quick as a lightning bolt that angel darts away followed by a small band. They rise above the hospital and begin circling. In the distance is a dark cloud that seems to be growing. It is getting closer and closer while the legion of angels pick up their speed resembling a streak of white brilliant lighting across the sky. A battle is about to take place. Hell knows there is something of eternal importance that must be stopped and they can spare no expense to get in the hospital. An heir of salvation must be stopped. In the waiting room prayers are rising. The pastor of the small church where Skylar attends calls all the saints at the hospital to join him in prayer. The sound of the pastors deep rich voice breaks the silence as he prays, "Father God, the creator and sustainer of this world, we humbly yet boldly come into your presence and past the gates of praise. We plead the blood of Jesus over Skylar. We asks precious Father that you touch her frail body and raise her up to your own glory.

With this prayer heaven in stirred. The Father sends the Holy Spirit to touch Skylar's body. Healing is taking place and heaven rejoices over the perfect plan of God. The doctors and nurses stand with eyes and mouths wide open. Not a person speaks and no one moves. The lack of busyness and silence causes Jackson to look toward the room. A small angel gently nudges his heart to walk slowly toward the room. He takes small steps and his heart beats faster and faster. He doesn't understand this strange feeling for this young woman he barely knows, but he is drawn to her side. He stops just short of the room as the doctors and nurses turn toward him. The youngest nurse smiles then motions to him with her small delicate hand to come closer. Without saying a word, her lips form the words, "come see." He walks closer and looks into the eyes of Skylar. The one who just hours before lay at deaths door, the one he held in his arms thinking she was gone, now looks back at him and gently smiles and whispers a faint, "thank you." It is at that moment the Holy Spirt joins their hearts for the purpose God has for them and for the future generations that will follow.

Outside of the hospital, as well as the old country church and Pearl's old run down house, dark forces begin to gather. Trajor waits in the top of the old giant oak tree just outside of the hospital, watching and waiting. Surmano and Ishnea keep their distance because they know the power of Trajor. They know he is planning something and he will do it quickly. The dark ominous cloud that was gathering has dissipated, but they are not far away. The legions that surrounded the hospital thwarted the attack, but did not stop what was to come. Trajor looks at the horizon and smiles a hideous smile then lets out a foul, disgusting laugh. He points at Surmano and Ishnea and then in a moment he is gone. Guards are set around the hospital room to make sure the healing can take place and God's plan for Jackson and Skylar can come to pass.

In two rooms on the second floor, Cindy and her family as well as Bobby and his family are trying to put together the pieces of the event. Bobby is broken and is finding it hard to speak. His mother tells him to calm down, but he can't seem to find peace and comfort. He tells his parents about the interaction with Jackson and how he taunted him. He tried to instigate a fight, but Jackson wouldn't fight back. Then all of a sudden the explosion happened and the next thing you know Jackson was picking him up and carrying him to safety. Bobby looks at his parents and says, "I made fun of Jackson for his faith. Every day he would talk about Jesus, but I only ridiculed him in front of everyone. Not once did he back down. Whatever he has I want it. I am tired of who I am and what I have become. I want that kind of faith in my life." His mom said, "Bobby, we can go to church next week if you want, but don't make a quick decision fueled by emotion. You have time, you're still young." Mom" he said, "You don't get it. I almost died today and if my life would have ended I don't know what would have happened. Today changed my life and you and Dad can come along or stay the way you are, but I want what Jackson has." Heaven goes into action and the Holy Spirit stirs Jackson's pastor to visit Bobby. The pastor walks in and introduces himself. He said, "I am Jackson and Skylar's pastor. I know you have dealt with a lot of things today and I just wanted to make sure you are OK." Bobby sits up against the advice of his mother and motions for the pastor to come to his bedside. He tries to speak, but he can only weep. The Holy Spirit is convicting him of sin and showing him his need for salvation. The Spirit gives Bobby believing faith and all of the sudden Bobby prays, "God, I am so sorry for the things I have done and for ignoring you. Please forgive me and give me what Jackson has." At the moment hell shudders and Trajor looks suddenly toward the hospital. The legion surrounding the hospital stands at attention and begins to sing a hallelujah chorus. Heaven celebrates with praise and thanksgiving, singing worthy is the Lamb. The Father turns to the recording angel and tells him to write the name Bobby. The Holy Spirit seals Bobby until the day of redemption and fills him with his presence. Today life has changed for more than one family and eternity is sealed forever.

At the moment Trajor calls for the demon of deceit and confusion to immediately go to Cindy's room. Already there is the spirit of greed and pride standing close to Cindy's dad. The pastor left Bobby's room and made his way to Cindy's room where he met Pearl and Jackson. Cindy's dad is uneasy with this group of church people hanging around and when the pastor asks to pray, Cindy's dad says, "Well preacher, where was your God when all this happened. Is he going to pay all these bills? Confusion does its best to get in to Jackson's mind. Jackson can't understand how this man can be so ungrateful. He thought Joe Kraft liked him when they were at his house for dinner several weeks ago, but now Jackson thinks it was all just a show. Jackson begins to speak when Joe puts up his hand and says, "Stop with the church stuff. All you want is money and donations. Well my daughter is not going to be a poster child for your gimmicks." Cindy is embarrassed and starts to speak when her mother tells her to calm down and get some rest. Cindy is now being prompted but the Holy Spirit. The angel of peace and grace hover over her. She sits up, slowly at first, wincing at the pain from her injuries, but she continues to pull herself up. Her father, Joe, looks at the guests in the room and says, "See what you have done. Now she is going to injure herself even more. Just leave our room, we don't need your mumbo jumbo religion" Cindy turns to

Joe and says, "Daddy, stop. That is enough. Jackson saved the life of your little girl and you can't be thankful for that?" She turns to Jackson and says, "I know what we thought we had was special, but I know now you were sent into my life to point me to Jesus. Jackson, how can I get what you have? What do I have to do to have God in my life?" The spirit of confusion is now really attacking this family. If he can only confuse Cindy and the spirit of greed and pride can keep pushing Joe, they might have a chance to stop this conversion. But greater is he that is in them than he that is in the world. Conviction continues to fall on Cindy's heart and she motions for Jackson to come to the side of bed. She whispers, "Jackson, tell me how to be saved. I was scared I was going to die today and I prayed for one more chance. Can you tell me how?" Jackson takes her hand and explains God's perfect plan of salvation. At that moment Cindy bows her head and surrenders to the Lord of Glory. Heaven once again rejoices and once again the recording angel is commanded to write the name Cindy.

Kurios is still waiting for his new assignment and wonders when it will happen. He was told it wouldn't be long and the way time is measured in Heaven, it can move very quickly. Just a little more time and Kurios will be introduced to his new assignment, but more preparation must take place. Kurios heard about Jackson and Skylar and that they were chosen by the Father to be together as husband and wife which is exactly where his new assignment will come from. Just a matter of a few short years and he will be given special charge over a new soul.

Time passes and Skylar is released from the Hospital. Jackson now is spending time with her and they are becoming close. The little church where they attend is now the focus of their lives and they are beginning to take a leadership role in the youth group at the church. The pastor has been praying for some help and the Father has been directing him to give Jackson some responsibility. After church on Sunday, pastor Eli Marshal, stops Jackson at the back door and asks if he can talk to him for a few minutes. Jackson looks at Skylar and Pearl as if waiting for direction and Skylar nods yes and smiles a big smile. Pastor Eli looks at Jackson and says, "Well, I take that as a yes?" Jackson says, "Yes sir as long as Skylar can come." Pearl smiles a big smile and says, "You both take your time, I am going to visit a little outside and then take my time walking home." The pastor closes the back door and leads the young couple down the aisle to a small cluttered office near the front of the church right beside the baptistry. It is a little musty smelling and the lighting isn't very good, but it is a comfortable room that has a sense of peace about it. Ishnea knows this place well because he has received strength from what goes on in this room. When he was preparing for a spiritual battle he would come to this place and watch the pastor give himself to the Lord. Ishnea has seen many battles won from this war room of faith. He always enjoyed just standing in the corner and watching this man of God commune with the Father. Ishnea watched as the Father poured out his favor. He remembers how The Father walked in the Garden of Eden with Adam and Eve and how much the Father smiled when he was spending time with a human who trusted him. Now Ishnea watches as this man hands out another assignment from the Father. But there is a strange feeling that just came over Ishnea. He leaves the war room and quickly darts outside to look around. Korsta has joined him as well as Kurios. These two angels look at Ishnea and asks, "What is it?" Ishnea stands tall and slowly raises his sword. He sees demons circling and then disappearing as if they are looking for something or someone. The angels circle the church to make sure no one is slipping in to interfere with the meeting and then go back inside, but not before Ishnea calls for a legion to be sent to this town to stand guard just in case Draden has something planned.

Back inside Eli asks Jackson and Skylar what their plans are after they graduate from High school in a few weeks. Jackson takes Skylar's hand and gives her a big smile then looks back at the pastor and says, "Well, we have been seeking the mind of God and we think we are going to start Bible college, but we are still not sure what we will be doing in ministry." Jackson continues by saying, "I don't want to go too far because Mama isn't doing that great and she needs me to help her out. I am going to get a job here local so I can help mama with the bills and take a few classes as I am able." The pastor turns to Skylar and asks the same question. She takes a deep breath and looks up and to her right. She scrunches up her nose and presses her lips together and then lets out the breath. "Pastor" she said, "I was sure God wanted me to be a missionary, but now I am not sure what that means or what he is leading me to do. All I know is I want to serve and make the most impact I can." The pastor bows his head and whispers something to himself then slaps his hands on both his knees and says, "Weeellll, I have an offer for both of you. God has been blessing this small church and we have a need that must be met. I have been praying and I believe God is telling me to ask both of you to help me here at the church. I would like you to take over the student ministries and build it while reaching students for Jesus. The pay isn't much, but it will be enough so Jackson can help Sister Pearl Mae and we will even help pay for your Bible college." Jackson gets a big smile on his face and looks over at Skylar. The Holy Spirit leans hard on Skylar and moves her heart to speak. He floods her soul with peace and assurance. She smiles and shakes her head enthusiastically yes. Jackson stands up and extends his hand to the pastor and says, "Pastor, I accept your offer to serve with you in ministry." Immediately Strago leaps to his feet and as fast as he can fly makes his way to this small church. He is followed by Trajor and Draden. Both dare not speak because they have seen this in his eyes before when David went to take a meal to his brothers while they were fighting the Philistines. Strago watched as David defied hell and without fear stood against Goliath. This has to stop now. Jackson can't be permitted to surrender to ministry. What little foothold they have in this town will be gone, not to mention the future generations that will follow Jackson and Skylar.

Strago tells Trajor that he is not to rest until he has effectively bombarded this young couple with doubt and confusion. He tells Trajor to immediately call in reinforcements and directs him to get the demons of Hate and Worry to begin doing their job on Jackson and Skylar. He also directs him to call in Praiger. Trajor looks at Strago and hesitates for a moment. Draden also remembers that name. He made an impact in the early church when he convinced Ananias and Sapphira to lie to the Holy Spirt. When that happened those two humans lost their life. He was really good at his job and these two young believers will be no match, but why such powerful demonic activity for a small town and two young people? It must be something important so they will pay close attention. In the meantime Ishnea is summoned by Micheal, the arch angel, to report to him. He immediately leaves the small church and makes his way to heaven to meet with Micheal while Korsta and Kurios continue to watch the show in the pastor's office. The pastor joins hands with Jackson and Skylar and begins to pray. In heaven, the legions of angels stop what they are doing and listens. The throne room's busyness stops for a brief moment as a strong God honoring, Christ exalting prayer comes to the ears of God.

"Father", Eli Prays. "Father, we love you and just can't get over how much you love us." The Holy Spirit pours out an abundance of grace and power at that moment and Eli receives boldness. "Father, in Jesus's name, I commit this young couple to you and ask that you open the windows of heaven and bar hell and all the demons from their life." What did he say, Draden and Strago are fuming and can't believe what they just heard. Strago slams his giant fist into the side of Trajor and lets out a long low growl. "How could you let this happen" If you had been doing your job that prayer would never have happened. Now we are banned and these two finite worthless humans have the power of heaven behind them. We can't touch them. The master is going to be furious."

CHAPTER FIVE

THE FUTURE BEGINS

Kurios is getting excited about his assignment and eagerly asks Gabriel about Dustin. Gabriel smiles and just stares at Kurios. "Let me tell you what I know." "The Father is planning a revival in the town of Prentice and it is going to be a very strong out pouring of His Spirit. It will be a time much like the great awakening under the saints of the 16th century and a generation will be shaken so much that the gospel will be given laborers in such amazing numbers that that the entire world will be touched. The reach will extend to nations from this one small little place called Prentice." Kurios is excited and asks about Dustin again. "Will the key be my new assignment?" Gabriel hesitates then says, "All that is in the Father's heart is not for us to know. We simply obey when it is time. Prepare yourself Kurios, and be ready when your assignment is here."

Strago has been meeting with the other generals in Hades army. They are planning for the next step and they can only guess based on the character of God and His Word. Strago remembers when Isaiah was prophesying about a seed out of dry ground and it drove him crazy. Why did God cause his prophets to speak in such riddles? It wasn't until the birth of God's only Son that he realized salvations plan was in motion. Only 33 years later would the battle take a turn they had not expected? They were there when the prophets spoke and they were there when God sent angels unaware. They just couldn't understand God's word, so they miscalculated and lost the battle at the grave. They will not let history repeat itself in this tiny little town. Strago looks to the west and sees a dark cloud rising. He stands tall and stretches his massive arms. Reinforcements are arriving and as they get closer. Strago sees two demons that have been effective in every great movement of God. The Spirit of Religion and condemnation arrives and stands by the general's side. They stand shoulder to shoulder and stare with a strong and united focus on something that does not make sense to them. They dare not enter this fight without all the facts, so they find a perch somewhere near the school.

Jackson and Skylar have been in student ministries for almost two years and they have been used to influence the school they previously attended, but something is about to happen that could possibly stop this movement. While everyone was distracted with the attacks against Jackson and Skylar they failed to see the demon of depression bothering Pearl Mae. Jackson doesn't know his mother has been battling cancer for 6 months and it is in the final stages.

Pearl lies in bed whispering prayers to The Lord, "Jesus, I know you love me, but I really don't understand why you stand by and do nothing. Jackson is faithfully serving you and now you want to take away his mama." In heaven the Lord is completing Pearls place. It won't be long until Pearl comes home and the escorting angel is standing ready to bring her home.

Jackson comes home and Pearl is laying in bed. She is weak and looks flushed, coughing frequently. She looks at Jackson as he walks in the bedroom and offers a small trembling smile. She doesn't cry but her eyebrows turn upwards and her lips tremble. She holds out her arms and uses her fingers to motion him to come closer. Still standing at the door, Skylar starts to cry. Jackson kneels beside his mother's bed and kisses her on her cheek. He continues this for several minutes. He whispers something, but Skylar can't make it out. Pearl looks at Jackson and then motions for Skylar to come closer. The Holy Spirit fills Pearl and causes her to speak for him. "Jackson, the Spirit of the Lord is upon you to preach glad tidings to all people. Be of good courage and hide His word in your heart. Do not turn to the right or to the left." Pearl is strengthened at that moment when an angel pours out a very special measure of grace. She sits up in bed and extends her hands toward the corner of the room. Her eyes light up and at that moment Ishnea and Surmano reveal themselves to her. They smile and she motions to them with a big smile. They tell her who they are and tell her what a joy it has been following her life and tell her they will care for Jackson and Skylar. The death angel then touches her and her soul is handed into the hands of the transporting angel. The breath of life is returned to the Father and she is whisked away. Her grip on Jackson's hand falls and her body settles down into the bed. At that very moment the power of grace overwhelms Jackson and he begins to cry uncontrollably. It is at that moment he realizes he is alone, but he is not alone. He brushes the hair back from his mother's face while Skylar leans against him and kisses his cheek. They stand and embrace sharing hugs and tears. Now, everything is in motion.

Jackson picks up the phone to call his pastor, but the Holy Spirit has already alerted him and just as the phone rings the doorbell also rings. Skylar goes to the door and when she opens it the Pastor reaches out and gives her a hug. Jackson stands just inside the door and is still crying. His eyes are red and he is breathing deeply, trying not to cry anymore. He just stands staring at the pastor who slowly walks toward him. The pastor stands in front of Jackson and grabs him by both shoulders. He doesn't say anything, he just stares. At that moment the demon of discouragement swoops in past Surmano and Ishnea. As they turn to deflect, the demons of religion and condemnation also attack. For a moment Jackson pulls back. His mind is overwhelmed and he steps back from the pastor. Jackson wipes his eyes and then says, "So this is the love of God? Taking my mama so suddenly?" Skylar speaks up and says, "Jackson, you know God loves you and your mama is in his presence." Jackson stares at her for a minute and then says, "I just want to be alone. Can someone call the police and make some arrangements? I am not sure what I believe right now." With that, Jackson quickly exits the back door. Skylar and the pastor hear the car start and the wheels squeal. Skylar quickly looks out the window and only sees the dust left dissipating with the wind. The pastor makes the call and waits for officials to come for Pearl's body.

Strago is celebrating. He commands several demons to follow Jackson to make sure he finds no rest. Discouragement leaves the house and follows. Ishnea and Surmano also follow, while a legion of angels surround Skylar and Pastor Eli. This is a critical time and hell cannot let up now. Attack after attack comes on Jackson as he drives faster and faster.

Pearl opens her eyes and when she does she sees a lone figure standing in front of her. There is a massive choir singing and the beauty surrounding her is indescribable. She looks and sees a throne that resembles a rainbow with brilliant colors. The floor is like crystal. Sparkling clear with no blemish. Surrounding the throne are 24 people clothed in brilliant white robes with crowns on their heads. In unison, in voices of comfort and peace they repeat, grace and honor and power to him who sits on the throne forever and ever. Hallelujah choruses echo across eternity and she looks and sees a sea of endless angels standing at attention saying all power and honor and glory to the lamb who was slain. It is at that moment she looks into the face of God. With a voice as soft as a morning rain and the power of a thousand waterfalls he speaks her name, "Pearl." She smiles and simply replies "Lord Jesus." They embrace and she realizes she is safe in the arms of Jesus. The Lord turns her around and shows her heaven. He then says, "Well done my good and faithful servant. Enter into the joy of your Lord." She begins walking across the crystal street and one by one the saints say hello. She looks and there is her husband, John. She instantly recognizes him and has an amazing feeling of pure love toward him. He is no longer her husband, he is her brother, a fellow child of God. Her soul is flooded with precious memories of her time walking on earth with him. They begin walking and she sees Moses, there is King David. She stands face to face with Ruth and Mary. There is Lazarus and Abraham. She walks and walks then blends into eternity.

It is dark and the car comes sliding to rest in a cloud of dust. Jackson is crying uncontrollably and can't see out of the windshield. He beats the steering wheel and begins screaming "I hate you. I thought you loved me. Why did I ever trust you?" Strago and Trajor are really stepping up the attacks. Thousands of demons surround the vehicle and Jackson is almost at a breaking point. Jackson continues to scream at God and hell is reeling with excitement. Just a little more time and this will stop. At that moment a bright blinding light splits the heavens. Legions of mighty angles break through the darkness and obliterate the demons. Micheal leads the charge and stands face to face with Strago and Trajor. He lifts his sword and with a mighty blow knocks them back. They respond in unison after they are able to recover. They use all their power to attack Jackson again, but there is a wall of angels surrounding him. The Father allows Jackson to continue screaming, but the Father sends the Holy Spirit to touch his heart. Jesus is moved and hates it when his children suffer like this, but he knows the present suffering will yield amazing power and grace. He lets Jackson live through it, but under his watch and protection. Jackson cries himself to sleep and dreams of his mama.

Morning comes and Jackson wakes up. At first he is disoriented and does not know where he is. He moves to unbuckle his seatbelt and the car moves. He looks and a ravine comes into focus. 500 feet straight down. The only thing holding the car is a large tree in front of the car and two large limbs that almost loom like two large fingers, holding the car securely. At that moment he hears a knock on the window and sees a tall dark skinned man in brilliant white clothes offering his hand through the open window. He has a gentle face and a welcoming smile. With no effort, he lifts Jackson from the car. Jackson feels like he is floating in the air and his spirit feels like he has never felt before. The man doesn't say a word, he just embraces Jackson. There is a peace like Jackson has ever felt before and he feels so secure and safe. He asks the man where he is but he just points. Jackson turns in the direction and when he turns back around the man is gone. All of a sudden a vehicle approaches and an elderly couple stops in an old dilapidated pickup truck. They stop and get out without saying a word. They walk over to Jackson who is still trying to figure out what is going. The old man speaks, "Son, what are you doing all the way out here?" Jackson doesn't speak but motions to the car. At that moment a loud crack is heard and the tree splits. The car breaks loose and topples 500 feet to the bottoms of the ravine. "Were you in an accident?" The old man asked. Jackson just shook his head and continued to stare. Ishnea and Surmano stand guard and make eye contact with another angel, Regallo. Ishnea speaks to him, "are they in your care?" Regallo responds by saying, "the Father instructed me to bring Bella and Noah this way to meet and take care of Jackson. Is he a special chosen vessel?" Surmano tells him the Father has a special plan for this heir of salvation that is not completely revealed. He told Regallo about the attacks of Strago and Trajor and the constant attacks to stop Jackson. Regallo, said," I remember talking to a small angel by the name of Kurios who mentioned this one called Jackson. Kurios thinks his new assignment is connected to this. Is it?" Surmano just nods his head and turns back to Jackson who is now getting into the truck with Bella and Noah. Without saying a word they turn the old truck around and start heading down the mountain. Bella looks at Jackson and with a soft voice asks him what he is running from and why he is mad at God. Jackson just stares and wonders how she knows. Jackson begins to tell them his story and how he just lost his mama. At that moment Noah pulls the old truck off to the side of the road and gets out. He walks around to the front of the truck and motions for Jackson to get out and join him. Jackson slowly gets out of the truck and walks to the front.

It has been 3 days since Jackson left after his mama went to heaven and no one has a clue where Jackson is. Local law enforcement have put out a BOLO for him, but no one has been able to get an answer. Skylar is depressed and her heart is breaking, but she knows she needs to tend to the business of Pearl's funeral. Pastor Eli made all the arrangements and it was decided to go ahead with the funeral in hopes that Jackson would be back before it starts. Pearl's small house is swarming with people from the church. Every room is filled with saints praying. Strago is in a panic now. He did not plan on this. He thought by bringing in the spirit of religion and condemnation, this group of believers would be defeated. Instead this man of God and this young woman brought the people together and now the power of prayer is moving heaven. In every corner of the room is a mighty angel with instructions from above to intercept any evil thought or intention and bring them under the captivity of Christ. Lucifer is pacing now and has become enraged at the incompetence of his followers. He storms through the air knocking demons left and right. Smaller demons hide in the shadows watching the rage and fury of hell as the saints pray and their faith is strengthened. Prayer after prayer goes up to the throne as a sweet offering. The Lord of Glory and the Ancient of Days smile as they watch their children take their place and fight the good fight. Tomorrow is the homecoming celebration for Pearl and heaven is getting ready to reveal the next step.

CHAPTER SIX

THE CALLING

Jackson and Noah stand at the front of the truck not saying a word. Finally Noah clears his throat, rubs his rough shaven gray beard and then says "young man we rarely come this way because it is too rough for Bella and me, so I am convinced we were sent here for you. We were praying this morning and both of us believe we had a special assignment today so we just started driving. We kept driving thinking we misunderstood until we saw your car. I am not going to ask you why you're here because I already know. Look across the valley to the other side of the mountain and tell me what you see. Jackson looks across the mountain and all he sees is a lot of trees and rocks. He scratches the top of his head and says, "Just a lot of trees and rocks." Noah clears his throat and says, look again. Jackson rubs his eyes and looks again. This time he continues to stare, adjusts his stance, leans forward and squints his eyes. Noah smiles and turns to Bella and winks. She smiles and folds her hands like she is praying. Surmano and Ishnea are there now and use their power to pull back the branches of the trees that cover the mountain side. Jackson thinks he is losing his mind as he watches this take place and just keeps staring. Slowly something comes into focus and Jackson begins to cry. "So Jackson, what do you see?" Jackson softly says, "A cross." Noah taps him on the shoulder and asks again, "what do you see?" Louder and with more confidence Jackson says, "A big wooden cross." Noah's turns Jackson around and asks him "and what do you think that means?" Jackson said, well, when I see a cross I think of what Jesus did for me." Noah said, "That's right." Bella jumps in at the prompting of the Holy Spirit and asks, "Did you see a person on that cross?" Jackson looks at her and said, "no, just a wooden cross." They both smile and Noah says, "That's right. As far as you and I are concerned, there is an empty cross and it isn't yours. The cross was yours until Jesus took it away from you and made it his own. Why do you keep acting like you have to carry it? Did someone special in your life just leave you?" Jackson stares at them then turns and stares at the cross. He whispers, "My mama just died." Bella now moves to stand in front of him and says, "Honey she isn't dead, she is alive, she just isn't alive here. She is with your daddy. Didn't your daddy tell you God prepared a special place for all of us?" Jackson's mind goes back to his daddy's old bible and the words his daddy wrote about preparing a place for us. At the moment the Holy Spirit fills Jackson and the same angel that poured out the golden vial of grace on his mama now pours out special grace on Jackson. He turns and hugs them both and asks if they know where the church is in Prentice. The both nod yes and motion for him to get into the truck. They can be there in about an hour.

People have been gathering at the church for Pearl's home going celebration. One by one everyone from that little town starts making their way to their seat. Kurios made his way along with Korsta. Surmano and Ishnea leave the trip to the care of Regallo who will travel with them. As Surmano and Ishnea make their way, they see a few demons here and their along the road, but they are really nothing to worry about. The big threat is Strago and Trajor. As they get closer to the church they also see Draden. They are not worried, just concerned. There is so much praise and worship about to be released that hell is worried a stand will be made today that will affect the church and the future of this place. Slowly the pastor makes his way to the pulpit and as he places his old worn Bible down on the pulpit everyone stops whispering and there is silence. In front of him at the bottom of the 3 steps leading up to the stage is a long white coffin. Over it is draped a small blue blanket and a picture of Pearl and Jackson. Skylar keeps looking back as if she is expecting someone, but there is no one there. She has not heard a word from Jackson for 3 days. She is crying now and can't seem to find any solace. In the congregation is Cindy and Bobby. Even Cindy's Dad is standing in the back of the church at his daughter's request. All around the outside of the church is an amazing sight. Shoulder to shoulder is a legion of mighty warrior angels standing with their backs to the church and their swords out of their sheaths. They shine like bolts of lightning and create a wall of light so powerful the demons cover their eyes and cower behind anything they can find.

Inside, a sweet old saint, Sister Nora, steps up to the pulpit and starts to sing, heaven stops as The Father and his son, lean over the balcony of heaven and listen. With grace and joy she begins, "Amazing grace, God's amazing grace how sweet the sound." She waves her hand in the air while looking up and continues to sing, "I said God's amazing grace how sweet it sounds because it saved a wretch like me. I once was lost, but praise God I'm found. I was blind but now I see." Silence again and Nora begins to pray, "Lord, thank you sweet

Jesus for your amazing grace. Father God, we bind together neighbors now and pray for Jackson. Father, bring him home. Open the windows of heaven and let us see with our own eyes the glory of the Lord. She continues to sing, "When we have been there ten thousand years shining as bright as the sun. We will have no less days to sing your praise than when we first begun." You can hear some amens and glories as she makes her way down past the casket to her place on the second row. The pastor stands and opens his bible. He whispers a little prayer for help and then reads "eye has not seen and the ear has not heard the things God has prepared for those who love him." He closed his bible and took a deep breath. "I know this is a difficult time for all of us. We know Pearl is home with Jesus, but we mourn because we don't know where Jackson is right now. I know God is in control of that too. If Our Father wanted to raise the lid of that casket and say rise, He could do it and Pearl's body would come out and walk around this church. The power of God could open those doors and Jackson could walk through those doors." At that very moment the back doors open and Jackson stands staring. Everyone looks back and no one says a word. Noah and Bella stand beside him. His clothes are torn and he has a laceration on his forehead. Skylar turns around almost in slow motion and sees him standing there. Their eyes meet and they both begin running toward each other down the aisle. They meet in the middle and embrace. Everyone begins to clap and shout. A few do a little dance in place and the woman wave their white handkerchiefs. The pastor looks up to heaven and raises his hands. Jackson takes Skylar by the hand and leads her to the front and stands next to the casket. He lays his hand on the cold metal and with one hand kisses his two fingers and then places them on the casket. Skylar reaches over to the front pew and grabs Jackson's daddy's bible. Jackson opens it to John

14 and begins reading. For a brief moment, the Father allows Jackson and Pearl take a peak and they see Jackson reading from God's word. The window closes as Pearl and John turn back to eternity knowing it will be just a short time until they see them again.

Jackson shares the story of the cross on the hill and how he gave his life to Jesus to follow him no matter when, where or how. He turns to Skylar, gets on one knee and asks her to be his partner in this life journey. She begins crying, wraps her arms around his neck and yells, "Yes" the church erupts in shouts and singing. A few run around the inside and the old gray haired grandmothers dance in place while raising their hands. The pastor stands with both hands raised and worships. Revival is breaking out. Walls are being broken down and people are hugging and crying tears of joy. Outside there is confusion. Not among the ranks of heavens host, but among the disgusting evil figures flying around just outside the reach of the mighty angels. There is fighting and arguing among them. Strago and Trajor fear the results of today and quickly call for a meeting to regroup for what lays ahead.

Jackson and Skylar start making plans for the wedding. They are limited on funds because neither one have much and Skylar's mother doesn't have anything. They look at their bank account and they realize after the funeral expenses they only have about $380 between them. They decide they will live in Jackson's old house until they can get a little ahead. They will get married in a small ceremony at their church and then work until they get enough to go to Bible College. There is no backing up now and the commitment he made to marry Skylar and surrender to ministry is not optional. God called and God will provide. At that moment there is a knock at the door. Jackson opens the door and standing at the door is Noah and Bella. Jackson is stunned, but asks them to come in. They come in and take a seat. They both turn to Jackson and Skylar and asks them what their future plans are. Jackson explains about the wedding and about college. He tells them he will start Bible college as soon as he saves enough money. Noah looks at him and says, "Well, that sounds like a good plan. Bella and I were talking about you both and you both remind us of ourselves years ago." Noah asked if he could share his testimony and Jackson shook his head yes.

Noah started by saying he met Bella when they were just teenagers and the minute he saw her he knew he would spend the rest of his life with her. They arrived without her daddy's blessing because he was a mean drunk and would do nothing except make their life miserable. Noah worked at a saw mill on other side of the mountain and they built their modest little home that they are still living in. They had been married for 2 years when Bella became pregnant and they had a little boy they named Will. They were such a happy family and lived alone in the mountains. Noah would go to work every day and the highlight of his day was when he went home to his family. When Will was around 10 years old a new family moved into the area and they had a son about the same age. The two became close friends and would spend every day together. When Will was sixteen him and his friend went exploring and never came home. It got dark and Noah went looking for them. He looked for hours and nothing. He had no one to help so he just kept looking. He was walking along the road where he and Bella met up with Jackson and stopped to rest. It was a bright full moon and the air was still. He thought he heard something but wasn't sure what it was. He heard it again and his heart started beating faster. It sounded like someone crying. He started down the mountain and the farther down he went the louder it became. When he broke into a clearing he saw Will's friend holding him and crying. He could see blood on the side of Will's head and his body was not moving. He walked toward him and took Wills body out of his arms. Without saying a word he began walking up the mountain with his friend following behind. He asked what happened and he told him they were running along the road when Will lost his footing. Will began sliding down the hill. His friend tried to stop his fall, but lost his balance too. They finally stopped and Will was leaning against the tree with his legs back under him. His friend picked him up and tried lifting him back up the mountain but they were both hurt pretty bad. On a rock next to Will, in his own writing was somethings scribbled on a rock, "forgive." He was so angry at that friend, but he could not get away from that word. He finally made peace with God and went to that friend. "Jackson, his name was John and he was your daddy. Both Bella and I have been waiting for this day since the time we lost Will. We watched your daddy grow up and marry your mama. We were there when you were born and we were there when your daddy died. He came back to that same place one day. He made his way down the mountain to the very place Will died. While he was making his way to the same tree where Will died, suddenly the tree cracked and a large limb fell on him. The very place where his friend died, he lost his life leaving a single mother and a small child. I took what was left of that tree and made the cross you saw." Noah looked over at Bella and she shook her head yes. Noah pulled out an envelope and handed it to Jackson. We want you to have this and we pray it will be what you need. Jackson opened the envelope and inside was a check in the amount of $100,000.00. Jackson handed the check to Skylar and she just stared in disbelief. Noah explained it was Will's inheritance and since they have no other family, the Father directed them to give it to him. In addition to this is the deed to a piece of property on the same mountain where

Will and John died. Noah said, "All we ask is that you allow us to live out our days on the mountain and that you dedicate that land to the Lord." Jackson stands and hugs them both and then turns to Jessie. At that moment the Lord turns to Gabriel and said "call Kurios. The time is near."

CHAPTER SEVEN

A NEW LIFE

The scene is tense and a multitude stands milling around waiting for direction. They talk among themselves and there is speculation about what this meeting is about. Some speculate that a new direction is going to be given or maybe someone will get promoted. A loud Shrieking sound stops the chatter and everyone freezes where they are. There is an extreme sense of fear filling this place. One by one the inhabitants of this place bow and back up. All of a sudden a creature enters in a display of power and authority. It is the one who was created greater than all created beings. He was, at one time, the favorite of the Father until the day pride was found in his heart. He tried to exalt himself above the Father and that is when God cast him from heaven. Thousands and thousands believed his lies and fell with him. All here realize the time is limited and there is little time to do as much damage as they can.

The little church is decorated with beautiful trimmings, but it is not extravagant. The congregation has prepared for this day and the entire community is excited about the marriage of Jackson and Skylar. The pastor and Jackson step to the center of the church from a side door and stand facing the back of the church. A soft organ starts playing the wedding song as Skylar steps from behind the door. Beside her is a small frame man dressed in an old dated suit, but his gray hair is parted perfectly and his old worn shoes are shined. His face lights up as Skylar places her arm over his bent arm. Noah smiles as they begin to walk down the aisle. Jackson thinks of the scripture that says, as a bride adorned for her husband. His mind goes back to the time he first saw her and how God turned his heart toward her when she was laying in the hospital. There is such an amazing love for her in his heart and he almost can't contain the joy. He begins to weep and thinks of his mama and how he would love to share this moment with her. He imagines what it would be like to have his daddy beside him at this time. He feels a hand on his shoulder and looks over at Bobby who has now become his best friend. Skylar stops in front of him and the pastor begins. Dearly beloved we have come to this place to see the hand of a God join this man and this woman in holy matrimony. The words begin to blur and the rest is nothing but words running together. Jackson can't take his eyes off of Skylar and she can't take her eyes off of him. They hold hands as their hearts are joined together. The reception is simple and short. Jackson and Skylar are headed to a small private home in the mountains owned by Noah and Bella. One of the members loans Jackson a car until he can get his own. They get in the car and drive.

With everything that has taken place in their life they are still rejoicing in what the Father is doing in their life. Jackson thinks out loud as they drive, "isn't it amazing how The Lord put Noah and Bella at just the right place at the right time? Boy was I lucky!" Skylar turns in her seat and leans her head on Jackson's shoulder and said, " you know luck had nothing to do with it just as luck had nothing to do with the accident at school, aaaannnd you are finally seeing how beautiful I am and how great of a catch I am." Jackson looks at her and kisses her on her forehead then says, "I am sooooo glad God is in control because I can't imagine being married to anyone else. I look forward to growing old with you and seeing our children grow as well." "Children" Skylar said, "Looks like you have this all planned out and you probably already have a name don't you?" Jackson laughs and then says "as a matter of fact I do." Skylar gets a serious look on her face and turns toward him with her mouth wide open and her forehead crinkled with a look that says are you serious. Jackson asks her if she wants to know and she said, "Well of course I do." "Are you sure? Ok. Our son's name will be Dustin." She thinks for a minute and then says "I like it." She then settles back down for the ride while she whispers a little prayer, "Father, I pray for our son Dustin and for his soul. I ask you send him to us and provide protection for him. We dedicate him to you in the name of Jesus Amen."

Kurios, it is time. Prepare for your special assignment. This will be a special charge and the Lord is going to pour out His Spirit on him. You need to gird up your loins and sharpen your sword. You are to immediately join Korsta, Reama, Ishnea and Surmano and let them fill you in on the plans. Michael looks at Kurios and says, "Kurios, this is a special assignment from the Lord and Dustin is a chosen vessel who will be used to turn many hearts and lives to the Lord. Hell and its army is stirring. They sense something is happening but they don't realize the magnitude. Now go and remember the power of our creator. Remember that hell and all its demons, including Lucifer, have already been defeated. All power has been given to Jesus and he has entrusted it to the joints heirs." Kurios meets up with his mentors and is thankful he gets the opportunity to watch these powerful angels at work. They follow the truck down the highway carefully watching over this godly couple as they travel. In a matter of days, Dustin will be formed in the womb and a life will begin that will change the world.

Jackson turns the truck off of Highway 37 onto an old dusty road. They travel down the dusty, rocky road and begin the accent up the side of a mountain. Jackson thinks to himself that he has agreed to something he shouldn't have agreed to. He should have taken Skylar to a nice hotel in the next town over. He starts to apologize to Skylar as they pull into an opening and see an amazingly beautiful log cabin. He stops the truck and stares. He looks at Skylar and she looks at him, then a big smile sweeps over their face. Jackson pulls out an envelope Noah gave him as he was leaving and told him not to open it until they arrived at the little cabin. Jackson opens the envelope and begins to read

Jackson and Skylar, many years ago Bella and I began saving and investing. Our plans were to retire in a quiet place on The top of this mountain. People told us we were crazy for buying this mountain, but we had a vision of using it for the Lord. When Will died, we thought our dream also died and the vision with him. This cabin seemed so lonely when we came and we knew the vision was not for us. It wasn't until we met you that we realized God's plan for this place. When you arrive, go to the old wooden shed on the northeast corner of the property. When you open the door look over your head and there will be an old red metal box. Inside you will find a set of keys and something else. We look forward to seeing the great things God is going to do through both of you and your child."

They look at each other and begin to cry. Jackson thought when Cindy and Bobby turned against him that he would never find anyone, then he met Skylar. He thought when his mama was taken from him that God didn't love him. He thought the accident was going to take his life, but God wanted him to meet Noah and Bella. He bows his head and thanks God that He did not always give him what he wanted, but always gave him what he needed. They both get out of the truck and walk to the shed. They open the door and look over the door and there is the red box. They take it down and slowly open it. Inside the box is an envelope with the names Skylar and Jackson. It was the deed to the house and the mountain which is approximately 1200 acres. Under the deed was a legal document that stated this property is dedicated to the work of the Lord to lead lost souls to Jesus and rescue those who are in trouble. Failure to use it for this will mean automatic revocation of this deed.

They take the key and walk to the front door. The cabin is a chalet style home with multiple floors. There are multiple fireplaces and in the front is a round room in the center. The middle reaches a height of thirty feet. The second floor has a large open porch across the front and a large barren tree shooting up in the front of the house. They open the front door and see a giant open space and at the back of the room is a big double wide staircase. To the right is a big open kitchen with a table that will seat about 20 people. To the left of the fireplace is a large room with multiple chairs setting in a circle with a small table and lamp on each table. They go up the stairs it is stops at a long hallway that goes right and left. The hallway has a banister and it overlooks the great room below. On the east side of the hall way is a series of 6 doors leading to bedrooms. Between each bedroom is a bathroom with a door access to the bathrooms. The house is about 5000 square feet with 7 bedrooms and 4 bathrooms. They go back down stairs and off the back of the house is a master bedroom with its own bath. Jackson and Skylar look at each other and then Skylar says, "Let's call it Will's place. Where dreams come true." Surmano looks at Kurios and smiles. There has been no activity from Strago or the others. Everything is quiet and at peace, but that has happened before. Kurios asks what is wrong and Surmano says, "Do you remember when the Lord was ascending back to heaven after he was raised from the dead?" Kurios says, "Yes, but what does that have to do with this?" Surmano continues, "The Church was at peace and there was an amazing joy and peace among the believers, but then the wicked one started working on people and it wasn't long until chaos erupted. The church began to be persecuted, but we all know where that went. We need to trust the Lord to make everything work for good. There are going to be attacks on this family and we need to be alert. Heaven has a plan and your new assignment is a major part of that plan."

Jackson and Skylar begin making immediate plans, but they realize there must be some preparation first. They promised God and told Noah and Bella they were going to get some formal training so they enroll in the Christian college in the next town over. They decide they will still go to the small church in Prentice and they will still help Pastor Eli, but God has something bigger than they can imagine. They decide to live in the house Jackson grew up in, but will make some modifications so it will be a little easier. They will fix the walls and add another bathroom. They believe this house will be a part of the future ministry so they will put a sign over the front door "Pearl's Palace." This is where they will study and plan for the ministry at "Will's Place." They are in their first semester of Bible college and are enjoying each other's company. Life is good and the Holy Spirit is using Skylar and Jackson even while they are in school. They have not told anyone about the Mountain and Will's place yet, because they don't want people to treat them any different. They know the value of the home and the land and do not want to put it in jeopardy. Jackson comes home from school and Skylar is already home. He walks in and throws his books on the couch while calling out for Skylar. As he walks into the small kitchen he sees a birthday cake on the kitchen table and thinks it is odd because it is not his birthday or Skylar's. When he gets closer he reads what is written on the cake, "Happy Birthday daddy." He looks over at Skylar. She claps her hands and jumps up and down. He says, "Does this mean what I think it means?" She nods and says, "We are having a baby!" The next nine months is s blur. School and working at Will's place on weekends then church on Sunday. They have told Bobby about the plans and he is all in. Bobby is going to school for business and has agreed to manage the business side when it gets to that place.

Kurios is elated and has been on cloud nine since the Father formed Dustin in the womb. It is almost time and he waits with excitement for the day Dustin will breathe his first breath. Surmano and Ishnea are excited as well, but are already preparing for what is coming. They are not sure what is coming, but they remember when Michael told them that the Father had special plans for Jackson and the generations that will follow. Korsta and Reama are also ready to assist and know that caring for Skylar and Jackson are just part of their assignment. The little house is a regular post for these mighty angelic hosts and they spend their time watching over Jackson at school and making sure Skylar is protected. Strago and Trajor have been lurking around for the past several weeks and have shown a special interest in this little house, especially Skylar. Surmano is uneasy and as he looks toward the east he sees an unfamiliar being. He is tall and thin and has a dark red tinge to his body. He is not one that moves quickly, but it appears his moves are very calculated and he is being closely watched by Strago and Trajor. They go towards him and stop just short of making contact, then move backwards as if there was an invisible fence around him. Surmano turns to Ishnea and asks if he has seen him before. Ishnea goes behind them to get a closer look and immediately a look comes across his face as he quickly makes his way back to the little house. Ishnea says, "Yes I know him and so do you. He changes forms depending on the situation and he is only called in when there is a possible threat of losing a generation." Surmano tries to identify him and then he suddenly realizes what Ishnea is talking about. "Is he the one that caused Cain and Abel to fight in the garden?" Surmano asked. Ishnea shakes his head and then says, "yes and he was also the one that was present when Herod killed all the babies when our Lord was on earth as a baby. That must mean he is here for Dustin." Kurios doesn't understand and asks a question. "Do you mean he is here for Dustin? Is he here to attack my new assignment?" They are silent for a moment then all of a sudden a bright lights flashes before their eyes. Michael is standing before them with sword in hand. He looks at Kurios and says, "Kurios, you have been selected to protect this new born child of the king. Dustin has been chosen by the Father to carry his name through difficult times and hell has taken notice. They are not sure what he will do, but they are not taking chances. They thought Jackson was the problem, but now realize Jackson is the vessel through which Dustin will come into the world." He continues, "be alert and always on guard for that one there. His name is Diablo and he is a master at destroying young lives. He has always caused humans to devalue human life and is behind many terrible wars and killings." They turn for another look at Diablo and see he has faded into the shadows. Their guard is up and they will be ready.

Skylar is at home and Jackson is at Will's place doing some work. Dustin isn't due for another week, but she has had a few small contractions. She calls her mother to come over to sit with her until Jackson comes home because he does not want her to be alone. It has been 30 minutes since she called her mother and she has not yet arrived. The drive was only 10 minutes so she is not sure what is taking place. Skylar calls Cindy and asks if she could come get her and take her by her mother's house. Cindy agrees and makes the short drive to the small house. She is met by a pregnant Skylar who slowly walks out the car holding her now giant belly. She gets into the car and they begin the drive to her mother's home, but something is wrong. As they take the usual route the road is closed off and there are multiple emergency vehicles blocking the road. Skylar strains to see, but the traffic is backed up too far. They wait and wait and finally the traffic starts to move. It has been an hour since she asked her mother to come over and she is getting worried. As they begin to inch up, Skylar's demeanor drops and her heart begins beating faster. She looks as she passes and she sees her mother's car. She yells, "Cindy, stop the car." She gets out and starts to run toward the accident scene. Kurios is immediately over her as is Korsta and Reama. In that instant, without any warning, Diablo dives in and causes Skylar to slip. Skylar falls hard and hits her head on the pavement. The last thing she remembers is a flash of light, then nothing. Kurios stands over her and is now face to face with Diablo and several other demons. Agony and fear attack the mind, but Kurios is giving his all to defend her knowing Dustin is in danger. How could he be so careless? The ambulance that was already on scene sends one of the paramedics to Skylar while the other one covers the body of the unknown female that was in the accident. Reama and Korsta stand by with swords drawn protecting Taylor, Skylar's mother.

That afternoon Skylar wakes up in the same hospital where she officially met Jackson and where she fell in love with her, except this time there is more at stake. The doctors and nurses are working at a frantic pace trying to figure out what to do for Skylar. She asks them, "What wrong? Is my baby okay?" They continue looking at the monitor and then orders an immediate transfer to another room. As they are preparing Skylar to be transferred, one of the nurses turns to Skylar and says, "it's the baby, we are getting a weak heart rate and we are not sure why. The Doctor has ordered for you to be taken to surgery. Is there anyone we can contact?" Skylar frantically says, "My mother." Cindy was nearby and Skylar looked at her and asked, "Is my mother Ok, I saw her car." Cindy looks at her and smiles, you mother is okay, but a little banged up. She is in the emergency room getting some bandages. She will be up in a few hours. About that time Bobby shows up and asked what's wrong. Cindy is about to speak when Skylar yells, "go get Jackson." Bobby runs out and jumps in his car and drives to will's place. As his car comes to a halt in a cloud of dust he sees Jackson on a small tractor moving some dirt around. Jackson waves and continues on, but Bobby runs over to where he is and motions for him to stop. Jackson says, "What are you doing are you crazy?" Bobby said, "Jackson, it's Skylar, she is in the hospital and there is a problem with Dustin. We need to get to the hospital quick" They get into the car and make it to the hospital in record time. Surmano and Ishnea made sure they traveled safe.

When they arrive they are greeted by Cindy and Skylar's mom, Taylor, as well as pastor Eli and several members of the church. Noah and Bella are there as well and are in the corner of the room holding hands and praying. Skylar has been in the operating room for 2 hours and everyone is getting an uneasy feeling. Suddenly a door opens and a tall, elderly doctor steps out and walks over to them. 'Is there a Jackson here?" Jackson stands up and says, "Yes sir, that's me." Everyone gathers around as the doctor begins to explain. "Your wife is fine. She had a difficult time, but she is okay." "The baby?" Jackson asks. The doctor puts his hand on Jackson's shoulder and lowers his head. He said, "The baby is fine, but there is something you need to know. He is a special child. Your baby has Down's Syndrome and a few other complications that are giving us some concerns."

CHAPTER EIGHT

THE KEYS OF THE KINGDOM

Kurios does not understand the Fathers plan concerning Dustin. He thought Dustin was going to grow up to have an impact on his world, but he seems to be the same as a small boy he remembers called Mephibosheth. He was a little boy that was crippled because his nurse dropped him while running and he was almost a throw away. Gabriel appears where Kurios is talking to himself and listens. He then makes Kurios aware of his presence and begins to speak, "Kurios, do you remember who Mephibosheth was? He was the son of royalty. His injury wasn't his fault, but he had to live with that. It wasn't until much later in life that he received the attention from King David that the Father had planned for him. If he had never been crippled he would have never been different and he would have never been noticed. Dustin is not abnormal. He is, in fact, supernatural. Humans are born into this world with all the normal faculties and they just trudge through life and take the design of our master for granted. People like Dustin are given special attention by God and they are formed in the womb by the special care of God. They have a very special and unique purpose and we have to be on guard because hell knows what is taking place. They are going to come with everything they have to stop Dustin. You see, he is an heir and joint heir with Jesus and he has the keys to the Kingdom. You need to realize Dustin is going to shake the world he is living in and you have the responsibility to make sure he gets there."

Strago is pacing back and forth near the entrance to the hospital. Trajor and several other demons are watching and wonder what has Strago so nervous. They are whispering back and forth when Strago stops and stares at them. One of them gets the nerve to ask and Strago screams at him and then takes a long hard swipe that lands on the right side of that demons face. "You imbecile, didn't you hear Gabriel, he has the keys of the Kingdom." The demon picks himself up off the ground and says, "But I thought all believers have the keys to the Kingdom?" "They do you idiot, but they don't realize it. This child has parents that are already using those keys and this child has a special assignment that is going to touch people's hearts and lives like we have not seen in a long time. Suddenly they all stop breathing and look to the west. Coming in the distance is a very large dark figure. Its speed is increasing and behind him is a bright red glow that leaves a streak across the sky. The creature circles once then twice. He gains height and speed then as straight as an arrow, dives toward the hospital. Surmano and Ishnea intercept but are pushed to the side. Korsta and Reama reinforce and for a moment stop the advance, but the power is so strong. Heaven knows what is happening and the saints in the waiting room are given a heavy burden. Pastor Eli senses something is wrong and his spirit is stirred. Prayers of faith rise quickly and powerfully to the throne and as they rise, demons fly in to intercept them. Satan's lead general makes it past these 4 guardians and is heading straight towards Dustin. Kurios stands upright and bravely braces to protect Dustin. He knows the power of hell is going to try to stop this. He braces for impact but it never comes. At the moment the prayers broke through two legions of mighty warriors of the heavenly host encircle the hospital room and this heir of the king is protected for the life that lay ahead.

Jackson is unaware of the spiritual warfare that is going on around him. His mind is spinning as he tries to understand what is going on. He slowly walks to the nursery where Dustin is laying in the neonatal unit. Jackson puts his hand on the glass and stares at the small frail body laying with tubes and lines attached all over his small body. Jackson continues to stare and while he is staring the angel of encouragement stands beside him and fills his mind with joy. The angel of trust comes behind and touches his heart and mind. Jackson begins to see Dustin in a different way. He falls into almost a trance as he imagines the future. The Father takes Jackson on a journey through time and shows him some of the things Dustin will accomplish. The Holy Spirit whispers to Jackson that Dustin does not need what other people do and he will amaze people as he grows into the chosen vessel he is destined to be. Kurios readjusts his stance and moves closer to Dustin's bed. He is now beginning to understand how special this assignment is.

Skylar stirs from her sleep and as she wakes up she looks over and sees her mother and several ladies from the church. She whispers, "Where is Jackson?" She turns toward the door and sees her husband standing in the doorway. She asks him, "Have you seen our son? I want to see him, please have them bring him in here." Jackson thinks for a moment how he is going to break the news. "Skylar" he says, "Dustin is different and I don't want you to be caught off guard." She sits up in bed and says, "I want to see him." She gets out of bed and stands up. She received strength from the Lord and begins walking down the hall. She stops at the window and stares at the small figure that is in a cradle just below the window in front of her. At that moment Dustin turns over and stares at her with big brown eyes. Skylar lets out a scream and everyone is caught off guard. They feel awkward and wonder what will happen now. Skylar begins to cry and then says, "He is so perfect and beautiful" She begins praising the Lord and thanking him. She wipes the tears of joy from her eyes then folds her hands like she is praying and touches her hands to her lips. She then takes one hand, kisses her two fingers and then blows a kiss toward Dustin. At that very moment Kurios touches Dustin and he smiles. There is a supernatural bond that will serve the kingdom well as Dustin becomes the one who carries the torch to Will's place.

This young family spends only a week in the hospital and the doctors are amazed at the progress Dustin has made. With the complications Dustin had at birth they can hardly believe he is going home. The doctor comes over to Skylar and Jackson and tells them a couple of things they need to be aware of. "Skylar, Jackson" the doctor says, "Dustin has limited eye sight and his hearing seems to be impaired. I just want you to keep an eye on him and bring him back for some tests later on after you get settled." They load Dustin in their small car and as Jackson straps him in he thinks of the words the doctor spoke and wonder if their dream of "Wills place" will have to be put off because of the complications.

It has been two years since Dustin was assigned to Kurios and he is growing in grace and knowledge. Dustin has limited eyesight but he has a smile that lights up the room. He is beginning to speak and when he does, Angels stop to listen. With his smile and the sound of his soothing voice, he captivates everyone that comes into contact with him. Jackson and Skylar are seeing it too and Dustin now controls Pearls Palace. Jackson has accelerated his education and is almost finished with Bible College. Just one more semester and he will have his Bachelor of Arts in Biblical Studies and thinks that is as far as is going in his education. The initial $100,000.00 Noah and Bella gave them is down to around $40,000.00. Pearls Palace took $20,000 to complete the renovations. His degree took another $15,000 and Will's place took $25,000 to improve the road up to the cabin and the clearing of some of the mountain. Bobby has been keeping it going by working extra hours without pay, but he can only do so much and the business side has had some complications with the business license and the insurance. Jackson is not so sure what the future holds for him and his family, but he will continue to press on with the vision for Will's place and the plan God has for Dustin.

The road is dark and dusty with very little traffic. Lone headlights appear on the crease of a Rocky hill slowly making its way to a compound on the edge of a mountain range on the eastern border of this Middle Eastern county. The lone driver looks over at his small passenger and then looks at his watch. There is very little time before the morning light creeps over the mountain range and illuminates his vehicle. If this happens before he gets to the safety of the border, it could very well end the life of his young passenger. He has frantically tried to arrange for safe passage for his son and he is hoping the contact made in America will be able to pull through. He heard of a place where his son can get the best care and can be protected. He accelerates the truck in an attempt to avoid the pair of headlights coming behind him at an increasing speed. Only three more miles and he will be there and young Joikim will be with people who can protect him. The vehicle behind him is increasing in speed and he knows he has to take evasive movements or it will be over. He ducks behind a large rock formation and removes Joikim from the truck. He wraps him in a blanket and places him in the crevice of one of the rocks, he says a small prayer of protection and takes off at a high rate of speed. The only way to stop them from taking him is to lead them away and make them think they have completed their task. He turns to the north toward a deep ravine known as the Camels Elbow. It is just off the road and multiple people have missed the road and fell victim to a fiery car crash. He turns the corner and slows just enough to take the chance of jumping from the vehicle before it drives over the cliff. If he times this right and with the protection from God, he will roll with minimal injuries and as the truck goes over the cliff he will be able to crawl to several large rocks that are approximately 75 feet from the cliff. If the light holds out and the men following him believe he and Joikim have died, he will be able to double back, pick up Joikim and make it to the border.

Strago and Trajor are still busy with trying to stop Dustin when they received word that heavens host has shown activity on the other side of the world and that activity is connected to Will's place. The master of darkness has assigned another general known as Cummano. He is the demon that was in charge of the Persian army that overtook Nebuchadnezzar. His tactics are well known and he has been successful in causing disruptions in the Middle East region. He is behind these men chasing Joikim and his father, Hakeem. The word was that Jesus has been speaking to Hakeem and they have been invited to participate in a new ministry in America in a small town called Prentice. Cummano is aware that Hakeem has hidden Joikim, but he knows only what he can see. At that moment, a band of angels show up and stand against

Cummano who is also surrounded by multiple demons. Reinforcements show up and surround the rocks where Joikim is hiding and stand guard as Hakeem is also still hiding. He watches the men as they stand and stare at the burning truck at the bottom of the ravine. At that moment a demon darts past several angels with the assistance of Cummano and is able to move a rock where Hakeem is hiding, one of the men turns around when he hears the sound and stares in Hakeem's direction. He slowly walks toward him with his weapon drawn and pointing in the direction of the rock. Hakeem prays like he has never prayed before and as he prays heaven causes the men to become distracted by a group of black ravens that suddenly appear from the ravine and flies directly toward the men. He turns to see the ravens just before they flew directly at him. He was able to duck and watch as the birds made a circle. This distraction was enough time for Hakeem to crawl from the rock pile to a ditch approximately 50 feet from the rock formation where he laid flat against the dusty rocky earth. His face is planted in the soil and his hands are tucked under his heaving chest. The man makes it to the rocks and looks around. Satisfied that nothing was there, he turned around and joined the other man in the truck. Slowly they drove away.

Hakeem slowly lifts his sweaty, dirty head just high enough to look over the sandy knoll. The sun has begun to rise causing an eerie orange glow to paint the landscape. The rocks begin to cast a long shadow across the rocky outcrops that stand like sentries between him and Joikim. He rises to his feet and scans the horizon and the area between him and Joikim. He begins walking with an uneasy feeling, but an assurance that this boy would be used by God. Hakeem makes it to where Joikim was hidden and kneels down. He slowly removes the blanket and looks into the face of his small child.

His hair is black as coal and his eyes are dark yet trusting. He looks at Hakeem and smiles. Hakeem pulls the child to his chest then sits down with his back against the large rock. He looks at Joikim and knows why his people have forsaken him. This child is different in the way he looks, but he is a special child in the spirit he has. In his culture a child with Down Syndrome is considered cursed by God and can cause bad things to happen among their people. Their custom is much like the ancient Spartans, and if a child is undesirable, they would eliminate that child. The idea of removing him from their tribe by turning him over to the elements was something Hakeem has seen before but he refused to allow to it happen. He grabbed Joikim before anyone was awake and left his village. He remembered a man he met a month ago that saw Joikim and told him about a special place God is creating in America. If he could get Joikim to that place, he would have a chance.

The physical world does not see what the spiritual world knows. The Father is constantly working and is looking for people who will trust him enough to follow him. It doesn't matter what country or village, He is at work and inviting humans to join him. The Father has his hand on Will's place because there is a world that needs what Dustin will give them. Much has been invested in him so many resources are being given to make sure this plan is carried out. Heaven masses angles in both places and hell sees this movement. Strago makes his way to talk to Cummano about the plans. They are not sure what is going to take place, but they know there is special attention given to these two children, almost like the child Moses.

Jackson and Bobby sit on the front porch of Will's place and don't say a word. They just stare ahead of them looking at the driveway coming into the clearing. Finally Jackson says,

"Bobby, are we sure we are doing what God wants?" Bobby stands up and stretches. He removes his baseball hat with his right hand and runs his hand through his blonde hair. He continues to stare across the parking area and finally speaks, "Jackson, from the day you stood up to me in front of my friends I knew you had something special and that has not changed. You need to check your emotions at the door and stand on the faith he has given you." He pulls out a small photograph and holds it in front of Jackson and says, "Take a good look at this." Jackson looks up and stares at a picture of his son, Dustin. His eyes begin to tear up as he look at this beautiful little boy with a giant smile that reaches across his wide face and reaches his small narrow set eyes that are sparkling like a diamond in the sun. He reaches out and touches the picture and at that moment The Holy Spirit of God touches Jackson's heart. Jackson wipes the tears from his eyes and says a prayer, "Father, I am so sorry that I ever doubted you. Please renew my faith in you and renew the vision you have given to us for this place. Prepare every person and heart that will come here and show us our purpose in what you are doing in us." Both men are now standing facing each other as they embrace with an emotion that stirs the angels watching. They pat each other on the back and whisper, "I love you man", then head to the truck to leave for the night. Tomorrow is a new day and with it a new hope.

CHAPTER NINE

FULL SCALE ATTACK

Morning comes early for Skylar and Dustin. He has been up and down all night and has been running a fever. Skylar has gotten very little sleep and is exhausted, but Dustin's cry pulls at her heart so she smiles at her little man and sings a little song she heard Pearls sing one time, "I am not alone I belong to you. Keep me safely in your arms just like you promised to." She holds Dustin and with a weak smile he looks up at her and whispers, "I love you mama." Skylar smiles too, but her heart is breaking. He looks so pale and he is so weak. Why would God give her this gift and then make them both suffer so much in the three short years of his life. Slowly Dustin drifts off to sleep not even realizing Kurios is just above him, watching him and protecting him. With a slight movement, Kurios causes a slight breeze in the room and then protects Dustin's mind as he begins to dream. The Father has sent a special angel to show Dustin what he will do and while showing Dustin, Skylar also gets to see.

The Lord reveals to Skylar and Dustin their special place in life. There is a house on the top of a mountain and surrounding that mountain are giants trees filled with all types of colors as brilliant as the most beautiful rainbow. In the middle of the giant trees is one small insignificant tree with small frail limbs and its leaves are barely hanging on. But this little tree has special powers. In each leaf there is a special power available to anyone who will take one of the leaves. No one wants to take the leaves because they don't believe, but there will be others, just like Dustin, who will find their way to this mountain and they too will have healing in their leaves. Dustin continues to sleep, but Skylar wakes up and is perplexed by their dream. What could it possibly mean? At that very moment there is a knock on door at Pearls Palace. Skylar lays Dustin down so he can continue sleeping. Skylar opens the door and there is a small frail White haired dark skinned woman. She has a Shaw thrown over her shoulder and she walked with a limp with a crooked back. Skylar and this woman just stare. Skylar can't turn away from the kindness in her eyes and the gentleness in her voice. Finally the old woman speaks, "Skylar, do not be afraid for the future. The big mighty trees you saw in your dream were legions of angels sent to protect Dustin. The small frail tree is Dustin and the leaves falling are for the healing of lives. People will come from all over the world to see and listen to Dustin and the ministry he will have at Wills place. But be cautious, hell knows about Dustin and at this very moment an attack is being planned to capture this special child because the demons can see the determination of the mighty warriors from heaven.

Hell meets with the leaders of this dark twisted group of creatures who at one time was special to the Father. One by one they arrive and stand impatiently waiting to know what will be taking place very soon. Cummano and Strago arrive in unison and stand before a large red hot, bench looking rock.

They stand 100 feet above the rest of the scrawny, disgusting looking demons who are so anxious they are fighting among themselves. Cummano lets out a low, powerful deep growl which catches the attention of everyone in the area. He stands up and speaks, "we have an important assignment that must be taken care of today. There is a child in the little town called Prentice and he has the hand of God on his life. Our job is to eliminate this child. We will at first go through the parents, Where is the demon of doubt and confusion. Leave immediately and attack Jackson and Skylar. Make sure you remind them how hard this life they are living and if God really loved them he would not have allowed this. The demon of sickness is already making progress, but Surmano and Ishnea are giving us problems. It is important that a legion stand between this small family and the Fathers protection. Do not waste any time, because heaven has something going on that will mean trouble for the dark kingdom. Hate and fear come here. There will be another child coming from another land. His name is Joikim and you need to intercept his travel. Do what you can to stop him from making it to this small town." Fear speaks up and says, "What can a small child do in such an unknown town?" Cummano leaps down from his tall perch and lands right in front of him. He slaps him with a vengeance and said, "Are you so foolish as to forget what happened when the Christ Child was born? You only created fear in the heart of religious people and that did little good to stop heaven from redeeming man. No go, take control and make sure you do everything you can to turn their heart into bitterness and anger." Immediately fear and hate are gone to search the skies for this one called Joikim. Little do they know God has assigned a very special Angel to protect Joikim and his dad Hakeem. His name is Nehojin and he is the angel of strength and victory. Hell almost trembles at the sight of

Nehojin just as they do when they see Micheal, almost, but not the same.

Joikim made it on to his flight to America. He is only 6 years old and also has Downs Syndrome, but the flight attendants have fallen in love with this little boy and bring him to first class. They start talking to Joikim and his simple wisdom and profound love and trust for God the Father is evident. He is a cute little boy with dark hair, almost as black as a piece of coal. His eyes are a dark brown and are set close together with dark eyebrows that move at the slightest smile. His lips are a deep red and press hard together except when he begins to laugh and then his whole face lights up. He has a little lisp in his speech, but when combined with his high pitched voice, makes what he says interesting and appealing. Anyone listening is forced to stop and listen. Leah, the lead flight attendant, takes a seat next to Joikim and asks him a simple question, "where are you headed and what will you do when you get there?" Joikim smiles a great big smile and sits up on both knees. He motions for her to come closer so he can whisper in her ear. "My daddy is sending me to a special place on the top of a mountain where I will meet a new friend, but my Father is sending me to help my friend help other people." Leah sits back and then turns toward Joikim and says, "You have two daddies?" "No, silly, I only have one daddy and his name is Hakeem. He is a rich man in my old village and he has many possessions, but the people in my village do not like the way I look and sound, so they wanted to make me leave the village. But My Father told my daddy to take me away so I can go to this special place in America. Leah, do you know my Father? He knows you. He said you are a very nice lady and he hopes one day you will believe in him." Leah's eyebrows turn down and her forehead shows creases like when you are thinking real hard and trying to understand something confusing. Two weeks before she was at dinner with a friend who asked her about her faith. Leah told her that she didn't know if she really believed in God, but would if he would only make it real somehow. Leah turns to Joikim who is smiling real big now and his eyes are wide open and staring right at her. He says, you do believe don't you?" Leah sits back in her chair and begins to cry. Her mind is spinning and her heart is opening. She turns to this little 6 year old and says, "How do I believe?" Joikim says, "You are believing right now. My Father is so happy that you are starting to trust him. Just tell him you are sorry for doubting him and ask him to take control of your life." Leah stops for a moment and wonders if she should just get up and walk away, but then she decides to stop this turmoil and ask Jesus to take her life and use her. At that very moment, heaven begins a series of praise and worship. Jesus turns to the recording angel and tells him to write the name, Leah. Her eternity is sealed forever and the Father assigns a special angel to guard and protect this new heir of salvation. Joikim leans back and claps his little hands and says to Leah with a lisp, ith is ent (isn't) it wonderful. I am tho happy for you."

Back at Pearls Palace, Jackson has just made it home and Skylar tells him about the dream. At first he is perplexed and is not sure he believes her, but then she pulls him over and makes him sit down on the bed facing her. "Jackson, I know there is something very special ahead of us and Dustin is the key to it all. He has been sick today and I am afraid something is wrong. Can we go in and pray for him?" Surmano, Kurios and Ishnea all draw near in Dustin's room. The Holy Spirit bends down and fills the heart of Jackson and Skylar. Their fear begins to subside and they find a deep inner peace. They kneel beside Dustin's bed and join hands. Jackson takes a deep breath and then in a soft, yet confident voice begins to pray,

"Father, we surrender our plans, our hearts and our will to you. Bind us together and hold us close to you. Give us your faith and help us to never doubt you. Fill our minds with your truth and our hearts with your Spirit." Ishnea and Surmano lean in closer. There is such power and beauty in this powerful prayer to the Lord. They lose themselves in the amazing powerful love and trust being displayed at this moment. They watch as the Angel of prayer gathers the sweet aroma of sacrifice and praise and turns to leave. Just as he is taking flight, Ishnea and Surmano see two dark figures circling in the distance. They can't get a clear line of sight, but they need to make sure this prayer gets through. They follow, keeping a close watch and leave Kurios to guard Dustin. They are almost out of sight when all of a sudden the demon of sickness makes a fast pass attempting to touch Dustin and cause him to falter, but Kurios sees him and immediately leaves Dustin for just a moment to counter attack. He stops sickness only feet way and pushes against him with all his might. It is in this brief moment that doubt and confusion make it from behind a dark cloud and land close to Skylar and Jackson. He touches their minds and begins to t fill their minds with doubt. Something is wrong and they do not understand how these two inexperienced and unlearned humans can resist. Jackson continues, "Father, in the name of your precious Son, I ask now that you command the demons of doubt and confusion to be banished from this place." At that exact moment a thunderous sound echoes across the expanse of time and a brilliant series of lightning cuts across the sky. Fear and Doubt turn at the very moment that this power of the most high catches them and obliterates their being. With a flash of light, fear and Doubt have no power and their influence is gone. Jackson leans over to Skylar and they embrace. "Skylar", Jackson says, "I love you with all my heart and I am so glad

God chose you to be my wife." Skylar picks up Dustin and holds him between them and prays, "Father, thank you for my precious husband and for this special child. Give us wisdom and understand on how to train him in your ways and to lead him to fulfill your purpose." All of a sudden a cool refreshing breeze blows through the room as the power of the Holy Spirit rests on them. They lay down, this small family of three, and fall asleep in a peaceful slumber with no worries or cares in the world.

CHAPTER TEN

WILL'S PLACE COMES ALIVE

Life continues on for this family and the town of Prentice. Joikim has made it to Pearls Palace and has been introduced to Dustin. Immediately this ten year old and this seven year old become close friends with a supernatural bond that can only be explained by faith. The two boys have a supernatural ability to move the hearts of people. Each Sunday they still visit the little church where Jackson and Skylar began their ministry and each Sunday there are more and more people starting to come to the church to see, hear and watch these two little boys. They have created a partnership where each one compliments the other and the power of God is extremely strong in their lives. The little church that once had sixty on a Sunday morning now has 180 in two services and every Sunday people are in the parking lot listening through loud speakers pointed out of the window. Many of the people attending have children with disabilities or mental impairments. The parents of these special children listen intently and watch with amazement as their own children respond to the words and actions of Joikim and Dustin. On one particular Sunday in late June the service was coming to an end and Dustin had just finished telling a story about a little man in a tree. This was his favorite story because he is little too and he likes the way Jesus looked up at him. Dustin bows his head and folds his hands to make it look like a church steeple. He begins to pray, "Father, I love my friend Joikim and he is my buddy." He looks over at Joikim and smiles a great big smile. Joikim turns to him and his face lights up and he leans over and gives Dustin a hug. Dustin continues, "I love him like you love me and everyone here. Especially that man standing in the back. Help him because he came a long way to see Joikim." The prayer stops and the entire congregation slowly turns to the back and sees a lone figure standing there with dark curly, almost greasy hair with a long black beard that covers his entire face. He just stands there and then slowly lifts his arms toward the stage. Joikim slowly stands to his feet and looks toward the back. He jumps up and down and claps his short stubby little hands tougher and screams in a high pitched voice of joy, "Papa. My Papa." He jumps from his place on the small church platform and with his awkward gate begins to run toward the back with his arms held straight out. Hakeem closes the gap as he makes his way toward his son. In the middle of the church aisle, Hakeem and Joikim meet and Hakeem lifts him up and twirls him around like they are dancing. "Oh Papa" Joikim says, "I knew you would come." Jackson doesn't understand what is happening until Bobby leans over and says, "This is the one I was telling you about. He is the one who will be funding Will's Place." The small backwards praise band begins to play an upbeat song, "Blessed be the name of the Lord, Blessed be the name of the Lord, Blessed be the name of the Lord almighty." The entire congregation starts to sing and people are embracing each other. Surmano, Ishnea, Kurios, Korsta and Reama are beaming with excitement as they watch these mortals worshipping their creator. Legions now have surrounded this small place and the Holy Spirt fills the air and the hearts of the people. All is right in heaven and Prentice today.

Right after the services Hakeem walks up to Jackson and Skylar. In his broken English he says, Me am, how you say, glad and bless to be in ere. My father is you father, yes? He tell me to come to place, here and give you money for special house for Joikim. At that moment a gentleman dressed in a long white robe with a sash draped across his shoulder and wrapped around his waist walks up to Jackson. He is a dark skinned man with a long dark beard and a chiseled face. He is carrying a dark brown leather briefcase with gold trim. As he walks up to Hakeem, he bows and motions a gesture to Joikim and Hakeem. He then says, "Master, is this the right time?" Hakeem Nods and motions with his right hand in a circular motion form his forehead to his chest. The man sets the briefcase down on a small table and begins to speak in a very distinguished and strong voice. "My master, Hakeem, Abdul, Joikim Haddad, wishes to honor you with a gift. He wishes to thank you for giving safe journey for his son Prince, Joikim. As a gift to you from his kingdom and from his Heavenly Father, Hakeem bestows on you a gift of 10 million US dollars. In addition there is a trust that is set up with a large firm in New York and they will distribute the additional funds as needed. My master wishes only to have a place at your table and to be a part of your "Will's Place." Jackson looks at Skylar and then at Bobby. Bobby is smiling, but he already knew that this was a possibility and has already checked on the validity of this gift. Bobby turns to Jackson and says, "I had a feeling there was something special about this so I took a chance with some of the money we had left and hired an investigation firm to check into it. I learned Joikim is indeed a prince of a small kingdom in the Middle East and his PAPA, Hakeem, is the ruler or at least was, until the elders and zealots wanted to eliminate Joikim because of his Down Syndrome. Hakeem has asked for asylum in the United States for him and his son. He has already established trusts in several accounts that are sheltered from his Kingdom." Jackson looks at Joikim and Hakeem and whispers, "Is this true?" Hakeem slowly nods and as he does he closes his eyes in a gesture of peace and humility. Will's Place is alive and now the possibilities are endless.

It has been 6 months since that day and the progress at Will's Place has been amazing. Noah and Bella are regulars with their own small private cottage on the back 20 acres almost at the top of the mountain. Jackson has made arrangements to clear a path down the mountain so their front porch faces the wooden cross Noah built years ago to honor his son Will and Jackson's dad, John. Each morning, both Bella and Noah will sit on their front porch swing and pray for Will's Place.

Almost all of the top of the mountain has been clear cut and there are now three more small three bedroom two bath cabins surrounding the main Chalet where Jackson and Jessie, Bobby and Cindy and now Hakeem and Joikim live. As you drive up the driveway and come into the clearing, you turn to the right and there is a large auditorium that will seat about 400 people. Its purpose is for people to come and learn about the God who has begun this great work. It has been filled on at least two occasion. The rumor around Prentice is that the media has been coming from all over the Northwest to learn about this miracle on the mountain called, "Will's Place."

One particular night everyone was sitting around the large kitchen table inside the main cabin, when a knock is heard at the door. It was around 9:30 and they all thought it was strange that someone would be coming up here unannounced. Jackson stood up and looked at everyone with a curious look on his face as he shrugs his shoulders. He went to the large ten foot high wooden doors of the chalet and slowly opened them. Everyone turned and stopped talking. They just stared without saying a word. Dustin and Joikim jumped to their feet and started smiling. The started to run toward the door when Skylar tried to stop them, but Dustin looked up at Skylar and said, "It's OK Mommy, she is our friend. They turn back and saw a disheartened woman standing at the door with a single suitcase by her side and from behind her was a little face with blonde hair and blue eyes. She slowly stepped out from behind the woman and gave a great big wide smile. He face lit up like a ray of sunshine on a bright summer day and her eyes sparkled like a pair of rare and beautiful diamonds. She had on a tattered white dress with daisy imprints and her worn shoes had ragged socks and worn shoe laces that would not stay tied. Dustin and Joikim ran up to her and gave her a hug and grabbed her by the hand then told everyone, "This is Becky. Our Father told us she would be coming to live with us." Everyone was floored and amazed. No one knew what to make of it not even the woman, so they just watched in amazement as these three special little people held hands and talked as if they knew each other for years. Ishnea and Surmano greet the new heavenly host that is there to protect Becky and her mother. Heaven's plan is coming together perfectly and everything is right on the mountain at Will's Place. Sleep will be sweet tonight as they await a new day on the mountain.

The next morning Jackson and Skylar awake to the smell of fresh bacon cooking and the aroma of coffee. The walk into the kitchen and the woman who came with Becky, is standing in the kitchen. Her name is Brindaline, but she prefers for people to call her Brindy. He face is bright and her voice is filled with Joy. She motions for them to sit at the places set at the large table and she brings them a cup of coffee and a plate with fresh bacon, eggs, toast and a piece of French toast. They look at each other and then at her. She says, "My name is Brendaline, but I prefer to be called Brindy. I guess you are wondering what we are doing here. Let me tell you my story and how we came to Will's Place." Jackson said, "Hang on a minute, you said Will's Place. How do you know that and how did you find it?" Brindy wipes her hands on her apron, grabs a cup of coffee and sits at the setting directly across from Skylar and Jackson. I came from a small town on the edge of small county outside of the Ukraine. My father was in the Soviet army and he met my mother who was a nurse on a medical mission trip. My mother was a believer and had a huge impact on my father. The fell in love and my father became a believer. It wasn't acceptable for a soldier to convert to a western religion and many did not approve of his marriage to my mother, but he loved her and they were thrust from his home country to a small village as a banishment. They settled in and my father became the pastor of the small church in the village. Life was good until our town was invaded by rogue soldiers of the Soviet army that left their assignment and were roaming the small country village stealing what they could including woman. I was attacked one night by several soldiers and my father heard my screams. I watched as they beat him and tortured him until he didn't move. Brindy began to cry but then took a deep breath, brushed back the hair from her face and wiped the tears from her eyes. I became pregnant by the vicious attack and because of that and because of the death of my father, my mother took me and brought me to America. I gave birth to Becky in a small town in the Deep South. The church we were attending was very judgmental and didn't think it was right that I was going to have a baby without a husband. Mama, tried to explain what happened, but they said, they really didn't care. They said the Bible is clear about illegitimate children and they could not allow such a family to be a part of their church. Mama was broken hearted, but she knew God had a plan so we moved again. Mama knew Becky was special so we began praying for Becky and her future that seemed so unsure.

Brindy gets up and grabs the coffee pot and goes around the table to fill the cups of Bobby, Cindy, Noah and Bella. She pours the coffee as she continues her story. Mama began to get sick and was unable to work as a nurse anymore so we had to move into a small unfurnished apartment in a woman's shelter. Mama started getting treatments for her cervical cancer, but the treatments didn't seem to help. Within three months of Becky being born, Mama went home to be with Jesus. I finally got a job at a local diner waiting on tables and was able to find a place for me and Becky to live. Each night a small white haired, frail dark skinned woman would come to the diner and stand outside just looking in. She had the most amazing eyes and she had a single Shaw draped over her shoulders. She never came in, but it was as if she was watching over me. Late one night, as I was closing, I saw her standing just outside, so I took off my apron and went outside. She turned to me and put out her small yet sturdy hands and took my hands. She lifted my hands and then looked at me and said, "Becky is special in the sight of the Father. He has a special place on the top of a mountain where you will find a home and she will fulfill her purpose." Then she said something strange that I remember so clearly, but I still have no idea what it means. By now everyone is sitting on the edge of their seats waiting for Brindy to finish.

Skylar looks at Brindy and says, "Well, what did she say?" Becky said, "She told me Becky was a leaf of a fragile tree that would be used for healing." Skylar leans back in her chair and runs her fingers through her hair while staring straight up at the ceiling. She starts to smile then begins to laugh out loud, harder and harder while crying big giant tears. Jackson pushes back his chair and turns Skylar toward him and says "what has gotten into you" Skylar looks Jackson in the eye and says, "It's the dream. It's the dream I had about Dustin. He was a small frail tree and his leaves would be for healing." Brindy stands looking in amazement. She then smiles and whispers "thank you Jesus, we are home."

Becky, Dustin and Joikim are inseparable. They almost speak their own language and there is never a sad look or word that comes out of their mouths. People visit Will's Place on a daily basis and spend time just watching these three interact. It seems most of the time they are talking to imaginary friends as they turn away from each other and look upward and talk. They are using strange names for their friends. Dustin speaks to someone he calls Kurios. Joikim talks to his friend Nehojin and Becky has a special friend she calls, Neejar. They will spend hours together talking to each other and to their friends and everyone has gotten used to it. Usually during this time Dustin will call out to his mom and tell her something his friend told him to tell her and his dad. She would stand amazed and ever perplexed when she heard what he was saying, but without exception each time he said something it actually had a huge impact on Will's Place. There was one particular time Dustin was talking to his friend ad he just smiled and said "OK." Dustin then went to Skylar and said, Mama, God said he wants you and daddy to go to town today and wait by the church." Skylar continues the story, "So we went to the church and waited for about one and a half hours. Just as we were about to leave a man came up to us and asked if we knew where Will's Place was. We told him we did and if we could help him. He said his daughter has been diagnosed with a serious illness that they say is incurable. She was saying her prayers one night and was talking to God like he was right in the room. She told him that God had a special place where she could go and get better and it was on top of a mountain. She said her friend told her to ask for Will." He said he didn't know where to turn but he heard a news story about a place in Prentice that was doing some amazingly good things. So he came to see if he could find it. Now every week his daughter comes to will's place to talk to the kids. Her disease is under control and she is living a normal life. In fact her dad has sold his business and is one of the main volunteers at Will's Place

But everything is not perfect. Hell has not forgotten this place and is still trying to get something to stop this work of God. Recently a group in the large city to the east of Prentice has begun a campaign to stop Will's Place. There has been an inquiry from the State Department of Children and Families about a cult using disabled children and religion to solicit financial donations. The Department of Revenue has also sent people to question the ministry about their books. Someone gave them a tip that a large sum of money recently showed up in the bank account and word has it that it came from a terrorist cell to launder money. Strago and Trajor have enlisted the help of some people who have no love for God and have been used in the past to disrupt the works of God. Trajor calls for the demon of religion to become involved and the spirit of poverty and deceit join in. One such person is a local banker who has befriended Bobby in order to gain access to the ministry. His name is Frank. He has been in Prentice for about four years and has made friends with several of the local pastors. The pastors have relied on Frank for loans for the Church and Frank has been quick to give unsecured loans to them knowing neither the pastors nor the congregations would be able to pay them back. His goal was not to make money, but to manipulate. Frank sets up a meeting with several of these pastors and Bobby in order to get to Jackson. Frank calls Bobby and says, "Let's meet at the country club. It's on me and we can talk business. I have several of the local pastors that will meet us there as well. We can play a round of golf and just let the boys be boys." Bobby agrees, but only because he believes the pastors being there will make it tolerable and maybe Frank can be an asset to the ministry. "Ok", Bobby says, "but I can only stay long enough to play nine holes and have a quick lunch, then I will have to get back to the mountain." Frank agrees and they set it up for 1PM that afternoon. The demon of religion leaves Frank and makes his way to the two pastors who are meeting at a local sports bar for lunch. Poverty and deceit come with him and all three stand close to where the two pastors are talking. Poverty reminds one of the pastors of his low salary and how he could do better. Deceit speaks to the other pastor and makes him think he is in control of his life and that this whole Jesus thing is really just a way to get people to do whatever he wants. They both talk about the plan Frank has to gain access to some of the money that Will's Place has in its control. While these men think they are men of God, they are in reality pawns in the hands of these three skilled demons who continue to work on them and manipulate them.

It is 1:00 and Frank steps out of his new Mercedes and waves at Bobby who is already standing at the door to the club house leaning on an old set of golf clubs. Just as Frank makes it to the door the two pastors come out of the clubhouse holding a beer. One says to Bobby, "Hey don't let this beer fool you, God said I could." He turns to his friend and laughs. The four men split up on carts and go to the first tee. They play through nine holes and the whole time Bobby is uncomfortable with these two pastors. He has never seen church leaders act the way they are acting and their language is really shocking. They say they need some time every now and then to let loose and get it out of their system and boy did they get it out this afternoon. Bobby prays silently for someone to call him and deliver him from this. As if on cue, his phone rings and it is Jackson. They talk for a minute then Bobby tells Frank he is sorry but he has to go, there is an emergency that he has to take care of. Maybe another day. As Bobby gets to his car he whispers a short prayer thanking God for the deliverance from that ungodly trio. Frank and the pastors go back in the club house and make small talk, but Frank is really being pressured by his hard and calloused heart. The demon of greed presses in on him and makes him furious that he was outplayed today, not in golf, but in strategy. He really thought he could get to Bobby and make an in road, but it seems Bobby has a different standard and this is going to be harder than it appears. He looks over at the two pastors who are watching a football game on TV and sipping on beer. He thinks how pathetic they are and how easily they can be manipulated. His mind goes back to a time when he actually had a little bit of belief. He remembers the pastor of his youth and how he thought he was such a loser. He didn't have a nice car or home. He always had something nice to say about people and he seemed to always give everything away. How could a man with any intelligence live like that? He laughs and then his smile fades away as he thinks about something that old pastor had that he has never had; peace. He rubs his eyes and scratches his hair in an attempt to avoid the thoughts that almost got to him. He would never be like that. He would never be poor or go without. This life is much better. The demon of greed smiles and is convinced Frank is going to be a big help if he can only keep his childhood memories at bay.

It has been over two years since the introduction of Hakeem, Joikim, Becky and Brindy to Will's Place and the word of this ministry has spread. Hakeem has become a strong man of faith at Will's Place and he is having an impact on people from his culture, but something has been happening that seems to have Hakeem on edge. Late one night Hakeem comes down stairs after saying goodnight to Joikim and stops at the bottom of the stairs. He looks out the big front windows and is startled. At first he takes small slow steps toward the front door. Jackson is over in the corner of the room reading his Bible as he watches Hakeem staring at the front door taking short calculated steps. Hakeem takes two steps then stops and stares as if he expecting to see something. Slowly he continues to walk toward the front door and his heart is beating faster and faster. Jackson laid his bible down and slowly, but quietly gets up and walks toward where Hakeem is almost frozen in his tracks. He walks up behind Hakeem and gently touches his shoulder. At first Hakeem is startled but he regains his composure and slowly turns to look at Jackson who says, "What is it? What did you see or hear?" Hakeem turns toward Jackson, puts his finger to his lips and then slowly turns back toward the window.

Nehojin is at full alert and got the attention of Surmano and Ishnea. They gather at the edge of the tree line where the road coming up the mountain breaks into the open. They watch intently, knowing something is going on. They see a shadow move quickly across the front of the large window, then a second and a third. Nehojin speaks, "great caution must be taken this night. It is the demon of terror and destruction." Kurios just arrived and heard the words of Nehojin then speaks up and says, "Who cares, he is no match for us. All we have to do is go up there and confront him" Nehojin explains the power of this demon. He has the power of Hell behind him and he was used by the wicked one to create distrust in the early church. He was sent to cause the great Apostle, Peter, to stand in front of his God and deny him. He is the demon that was used to make the disciples run and hide in fear. He is the demon that led the start of WWII. If he is here then something serious is getting ready to take place. Word spreads quickly and heaven is stepping up the level of protection so Will's Place will not experience a setback. Nehojin moves to a strategic position just above the front door where he can see Hakeem and Joikim's room. Surrounding the perimeter of the chalet are approximately 100 mighty warriors of the heavenly host standing at attention with their swords by their side. They are always attentive to every motion and sound. Inside the chalet, Hakeem sits down at the kitchen table, folds his hands and begins to pray, "Father, I am in your hands and do not worry about what might come in your service. I only ask for the grace to accept your perfect will in my life even if I can't see or understand." The Holy Spirit touches his heart and fills it with grace and understanding. At that very moment the joy of the Lord fills his heart and mind and fear flees from him. Outside Nehojin relaxes just a little as he checks the perimeter of the mountain and does not see any sign of the demon of Terror and destruction. His name is Boraga and he is not far away.

In spite of all the spiritual darkness surrounding the area, Will's place is making amazing strides. Every Saturday and Sunday, large groups are coming to the mountain. Becky, Joikim and Dustin are making an impact on the people coming and are motivating families to reach for their God given dreams. Every family that comes has a special child that the world has given up on but each child has a God given purpose. This coming Saturday evening is going to be special. There is a family that will be meeting with destiny even though they think they are just coming for a couple of days to get a way and give their twins a chance to make a memory. These two children have had a hard life. They were joined at the hips at birth and their medical complications has been overwhelming, but in spite of that they are always looking for the bright side. One week before coming to Will's Place, Jerry and Kerry were at home just laying in the backyard listening to music when all of a sudden there was a strong wind. The Dad, Jason, was watching from the large back window when all of a sudden a large limb broke off top of a very large Live Oak tree in the back yard. He watched the limb come crashing down toward Kerry and Jerry. It seemed as though time stood still and everything was in slow motion. The twins didn't see the limb as it began descending toward them. At that very moment something hit the large glass window and shattered it into a thousand pieces causing Jason to lose sight of the twins. When he recovered, the twins were gone and all he could see were their legs sticking out from under the green foliage. He runs as fast as he can to where the twins were laying and begins pulling back the limbs to reveal the two twins still laying there listening to music. They turned towards Jason and both of them smiled. Kerry said, "Daddy don't cry, Jesus said we are going to a mountain where we will make new friends." At that moment Jason sensed the presence of God and wondered in his heart what was going on in his life and the life of the twins. Where this mountain and what is so special. On the other side of town a man and his family are watching television when a commercial comes on that gets his attention. It is a scene with three children with Down's Syndrome. The one in the middle has a captivating smile and soothing voice. They are standing arm in arm and behind them is a beautiful chalet. The little boy with blonde hair and blue eyes, begins to speak. The man tells everyone to be quiet and listen, "Hi my name is Dustin and these are my friends, Joikim and Becky. We want to invite you to Will's place on the top of the mountain just outside of the Town of Prentice on County Road 37. This is a special place for families and their special children. God told me to tell you to come see us. Jeff, he told me he has something special for you." "Honey, did you hear what he said?" His wife turned and looked at him with surprise and said "did he say Jeff? Did he use your name?" Jeff stands up and looks at the TV then turns to his own daughter who is sitting in a wheel chair with her hands folded together. He turns to Jamie and she is smiling from ear to ear, "Daddddddy, caaaan, weeeee gogogogogo go?" "Yes baby we can go, we will leave first thing in the morning. Let me call the office and cancel my appointments." He picks up the phone and says, "Hi, this is Dr Jeff Sinclair, I want to cancel all my appointments tomorrow. Please call my partner, Dr Welch if you have an emergency."

It's Friday night and Kerry and Jerry are excited about going to the mountain. Their dad located Will's place and is making arrangements to leave in the morning. Having twins still joined together makes traveling a difficult process, but it is one they have become accustomed to and have also become proficient in the process. Jason has been praying for an operation that would separate the twins, but the cost is too much for him to afford on an electrician's salary and their mother barely makes any thing as a school teacher. Maybe tomorrow the twins will find some friends that will make their life easier to bear. He can only pray. He puts the twins to bed but they are chattering a mile a minute. Jason tells them it is time to pray so Kerry prays for both of them. "Jesus I am so happy that you are taking us to see Dustin and Becky and Joikim. Tell them we will see them tomorrow and thank you that you are going to help me and Jerry to have the surgery so we can run and play. Daddy said to tell you Hi and would you please tell him it will be okay. Please tell him he doesn't have to cry." Jason wipes the tears from his eyes and his wife, Lauren, walks up behind him, puts her head on his shoulders and wraps her arms around his waist. He looks back and gives her a weak, broken hearted smile and offers his cheek for a soft kiss. She kisses his cheek and says, "Tomorrow will be a special day for our special family. I believe God has a blessing that will change our lives" They lean over and kiss Kerry and Jerry then step toward the door, turn off the light and watch the two children as they make their awkward adjustment so they can sleep. In the corner of the room are two special angels watching over the two children. They settle in for the night and as they do, Jason and Lauren could swear they saw Kerry and Jerry turn toward the corner of their room and say, "Thank you for watching over us." Jason and Lauren thought they were speaking to them, but the angels simply smile back as they watch these special heirs of salvation.

Morning comes quickly as the two families make preparations to leave for Will's Place. Dr Sinclair and his wife, Josie, load Jaimie into the special equipped van and as they are pulling out of the driveway, Jamie begins to sing, "Jeeeessus, looooovvves me. Jessssssussss loveeeeees me, I knknknoooow he lllllooves me." Robert and Josie smile and thank God their daughter is experiencing such joy. On the other side of the state another family is on their way as well. Kerry and Jerry are strapped into their special seat and are excited. They clap their hands awkwardly together and start singing as well. "He's got the whole world in his hands, he has the whole world in his hands." Jerry stops and says, "Momma and daddy, sing with us." They all begin to sing as they are driving down the road to this special destination. Kerry stops for a moment and said, "Daddy, do you know what God told me last night?" Jason responds, "What did he tell you sweetheart?" Kerry gives a loud giggle and then says, "Jesus told me he is going to let us have the operation so me and Jerry can run and play." Lauren looks at Jason and shrugs her shoulders and says, "We can only pray."

Meanwhile at Will's place the mountain is coming alive. Cars are lining the roadway and they are bumper to bumper coming up the 1.2 mile drive up the mountain. The parking lot is filling up and as car doors are opening, children start coming out of those cars, laughing and talking. The children are acting like every other child is their best friend and they immediately hold hands and dance together. Without waiting for their parents they start running toward the front of the meeting hall, which is a big giant barn type building. Some of the children are in wheel chairs while some of them are wearing braces making their ability to walk mechanical and slow. But the ones who can walk wait on the ones who can't. Children are even starting to push the wheel chairs toward the front. As if on que they all start singing Jesus loves me. When they arrive at the front door, Dustin Joikim and Becky are standing at the door clapping their hands and telling everyone to come on in. As the children enter the building they see beautiful colorful lights with a long hall way in the middle. On either side of the hall are rooms filled with places to play, but these are special rooms. The playground equipment is low to the ground and is designed in such a way that a wheel chair can enter the maze. At each ramp is a volunteer with a bright shirt and a funny looking hat with a tassel hanging on one side. As the children approach, the volunteers give them a high five and a big smile as they help them play at Will's Place.

The energy is amazing and the joy on the children's faces is electrifying. There are hallways along the outside walls of the building with benches so the parents can safely watch their children play. It seems like this is a little heaven on earth and even the hard hearted parents who have been bitter at God for what he allowed are starting to smile again. The power of the Holy Spirt and the freedom of worship is being released. The heavenly hosts are rejoicing and the praise of the saints moves creation. The entire mountain comes alive and with the enormous amount of praise, there is a stirring of hell that is building and looking for the chance to stop this movement of God.

Dr Sinclair arrives and right next to him another vehicle parks. He looks inside the back window and he sees two little heads sticking up and with big smiles on their faces. He watches as the big side door opens and two children step out. Their eyes meet and the children smile as Dr Sinclair says hi. Kerry smiles and then turns to her daddy and says, "Daddy, see that nice man? He is going to help us?" Dr Sinclair just stands there amazed and wonders who arranged this meeting. How did they know he would be here, how did they park next to him and how did they know what he did for a living. He turns and opens the door and Jaimie rolls her wheel chair out. Jerry and Kerry are standing at the bottom of the ramp and when the wheel chair stops Jaimie smiles at them and then turns to her daddy and says, "Daddy, Jesus said you are going to help them. Are you?" Jason and Lauren are standing there wondering what is going on. Jeff looks at her with tears in his eyes then turns to Jason and Lauren and says, "Hi, I'm Dr. Jeff Sinclair. I am the head of neurology at St James Hospital and I specialize in separating twins. How can I be of assistance?" Jason's jaw drops and Lauren puts her hands over her mouth and begins to cry. Jason just stares for a minute then speaks,

"I'm sorry, there must be a misunderstanding. I am confused. How did you find out we were going to be here?" Dr Sinclair says, "I really don't know. My Daughter wanted to come here so we are here. Can I ask why you haven't sought medical help for your twins, I haven't seen you at the hospital." Jason leans against his vehicle and says, "Dr Sinclair is it? We have been to the hospital, but we have been told our insurance will not cover the surgery and we don't have the money to begin the process so we were never able to get a consultation?" Dr. Sinclair is now being moved with compassion. His wife looks at him and softly shakes her head yes, Dr Sinclair reaches into his pocket and retrieves a business card and hands it to Jason, "Here, take this and bring the Twins to my office Monday morning and we will see what can be done." There is instant bonding between the families as Jerry and Kerry take the handles of Jaimie's wheel chair and start pushing her toward the front door.

CHAPTER ELEVEN

DUSTIN TAKES HIS PLACE

In a dimly lit office on the top floor of an office building in a large town, four men sit at a long mahogany table with 12 leather bound chairs neatly aligning the expensive conference table. In each corner of the room are dark foreboding figures unseen by the men who are meeting, but their influence is definitely being felt. They are the demons of greed, disruption, depression and hate. All four are nervously waiting for the conversation to get to the point. Hate is becoming impatient and starts to move to twist the minds of these men, but depression reminds them of their instructions. "Strago said to wait for the right moment and influence their thoughts at just the right moment. Now is not the time to make them hate. We need to get them to think about the money and the power that is waiting to be taken. We don't need them to be blinded by the hate that will come in time." The four men pour another drink into their small crystal glasses and just sit in the dark. Finally one of them begins to speak, "Frank, what did you say was the net worth of that place, what is it Wiley's place?" Frank puts down his glass and wipes his mouth with a monogrammed handkerchief and says, "It's Will's Place and I didn't say what it was worth, but if you want to know the worth I can tell you what I know. On old man and woman gave them the chalet and the mountain, the entire mountain it sits on. He gave them $100,000 dollars to begin building. When they got down to $40,000 someone named Hakeem, gave them ten million and a firm in New York has a trust set up with almost bottomless pockets." One of the men, an elderly man with white hair and a distinguished profile, leans back in his chair and rubs his chin then clears his throat. "Frank is it? What name did you use? Did you say Hakeem? Frank nods his head yes and then stares at the elderly man. The other two look at Frank then look back at the old man. One of the other man asks him what that means. The elderly man said, "I have been involved in international finance and I know someone by that name, but surely it can't be him. Frank, do you know his full name?" Frank opens up his briefcase and takes out a Manila folder. He opens it and shuffles a couple of papers then takes one out of the pile, "His name is Hakeem, Abdul, Joikim Haddad." All three men then look at the elderly man who stands and walks over to the large window overlooking the city. "The last time I heard that name I was in a meeting of a worldwide finance company that deals with the top 500 wealthiest men in the world and that man was on that list. Gentlemen, that ministry on that mountain has almost unlimited financial resources." Greed jumps from his perch and lands on the shoulder of Frank and whispers in his ear. He then moves to the other two and causes their mind to wonder about the possibilities. Hate goes over to the elderly man and attacks his mind. He reminds the old man of the future he almost had until that man stole it from him by putting so much into that deformed son of his. He lost millions and he has nothing but disdain for Hakeem.

Depression then presses on his mind and when combined with greed and hate, his hard heart is stirred. He turns back and says, "Gentleman, we have to do something and do it now."

At Will's Place Dustin has become a strong advocate for children who don't have anything the world wants, but he is convinced they have what the world needs. Dustin is now 10 years old and it has been 3 years since that meeting between the four mysterious men in that top poorly lit office. God the Father has been working special miracles and Dustin is now taking his place among the spiritual leaders. He is only 10 years old, but his knowledge of scripture is supernatural and his spirituality is many years beyond his age. He prays constantly and when he speaks it is as if Jesus himself is speaking. He is humble yet confident and his demeanor is that of a warrior general. His two friends, Joikim and Becky are usually beside him, except when he sneaks away to spend time alone with God. Usually around 5PM Dustin will walk out of the house and go to a special place on the very top of the mountain. It is a special place with a small shed like building with large panes of glass on each of the hexagon sides. The roof is metal except at the very top is a clear piece of glass. He locks himself in and prays for hours. Stationed around this prayer room are very strong, powerful angels and inside is Dustin's angel, Kurios. On this night Dustin will have an encounter with His God that could be compared to the time Moses was on the Mountain with God and received God's Ten Commandments. Dustin stands with his short stubby little hands, attached to short thick arms, lifted toward the heavens. "Father, I love you so much and I am really, really glad you love me. I want to be your best person on earth to tell everyone about you. Thank you for making me like I am. If I was making me, I would do it just like you did. I know there is evil wanting to stop your plan for Will's Place. I have seen some of the fallen angels staying around our house and one of them even kept working on me. Thank you for Father for Kurios." He turns and looks in the corner and says, "Hi Kurios, thank you for helping me." Kurios is nervous because humans are not supposed to be able to see him, but Dustin is someone special. Dustin continues to pray and as he does there is a stirring of slumbering spirits that were once silent. Now there is a strong desire to counteract faith.

It's now 8:00 and the door opens. Dustin and Jackson walk in and everyone sitting at the big table turns toward the door. Becky and Joikim jump up and run over to the door, but stop short and just stare. Everyone at the table is silent and Jackson, standing behind Dustin, is wondering what is going on. Skylar stands and slowly walks toward the door. She motions for Jackson to walk towards her. Jackson pats Dustin on the head and saunters over to where Skylar is standing and gives her a kiss on the cheek. She offers her cheek, but never takes her eyes off of Dustin. Jackson says, "What is going on what are…." Jackson also is speechless and just stares. Dustin is standing in front of them and it looks like his entire body is glowing. The room is brightly lit, but his countenance is almost as bright as the noon day sun. Dustin gives a great big smile and then says, "Daddy, mama, I saw my Father tonight in my prayer shed. He said I couldn't look at his face, but he said I could watch as he passed by me. I felt something touch my head and then when I opened my eyes, there He was. He was as bright as the brightest sun in the middle of the summer. He looked like there were rainbows all around him and the place where he walked looked like pure gold. Kurios smiled at me after he left and told me I was doing well. He told me to just keep trusting my Father." Jackson walked toward him and said, "Who is Kurios?" Dustin smiles then says, "Oh he is my special angel. My Father told him he was doing well and he smiled at me again." My Father told me that Will's Place is going to change the world and he will give us everything we need. Hakeem, he told me to tell you thank you for trusting him enough to give the money to Will's Place and he said to tell you Joikim is special to Him and He will protect him." Hakeem leans back in his chair with his eyes and mouth wide open. Joikim comes over to him and stands in front of him. Hakeem is crying now so Joikim climbs up in his lap and wipes the tears away and says, "Papa, God really does love us. I am so glad you are my Papa." Dustin makes his way to the table, sits down and begins to tell them the plans the Father has for Will's Place. Everyone is amazed at the wisdom and insight of this ten year old. It is obvious he has been with God.

No one is able to sleep. They sit and listen to Dustin as he explains God's plans. "My father told me children from all over the world will be coming to Will's place. There will be children and their families who have been thrown away by the world, but he made them special and he has plans for each of them so he will bring them here. Father said we are supposed to build 12 houses on the mountain with 6 bedrooms and 6 baths for each of the families that will come to stay. They will stay for 6 months and then he will use us to help them start another will's place in their country. Father said there will be people who are coming to try to stop his work here, but do not be afraid of them, He will send many angels to help us and he said he has many powerful people he has placed in important positions that he will empower to help us. Daddy, father also said to tell you John and pearl are OK and they will be waiting for you when you come home, but he said it will be a long time before you see them. Mama, God said he loves you and he handpicked you to be my mama. DO not be afraid and he said you should smile more when you talk to him. Joikim, he really loves you a lot and said you are going to lead many of your people to him when you go back to your country with your Papa. Bobby and Cindy, he is very proud of you and he said he is going to give you a special little boy of your own who will help us at Will's place. Noah and Bella, Father wanted me to tell you Will is with him and he is sorry he took him so early, but he is proud of the way you didn't get mad at him. He has prepared a place for you and Will is waiting for you. They listen for hours as Dustin lays out God's plans for the future. Right outside is a messenger from hell listening to bring news back to the prince of Darkness. Angels stand by wondering why the Father would allow the evil one to know the plans, but Dustin is aware and when he looks out the window smiles at that demons who shudders with fear at this child.

Word has gotten to some powerful people in Washington who are concerned about this unknown sleepy little town and something that is happening on the top of a mountain in the upper Midwest. The ACLU has been pulling some strings and there is an investigation being started about the things going on there and the possible exploitation of children, especially children with special needs. Frank gets a call from the elderly gentleman that he met three years ago and asks for another meeting, this time in the nation's capital. Franks get an email with airline reservations and arrangements for accommodations. He leaves Friday morning and will be picked up at the Washington airport. After he prints out his boarding passes and his itinerary, he walks over to his 20th story window and sips the bourbon in his glass. His mind is being flooded with the possibilities of this meeting. The demon of greed and the demon of fame jump at the chance to get their talons in his mind. They show him all the possibilities that will be available to him and how profitable it will be. Little does he know he is a pawn in the game of eternal chess and he is about to jump in with his whole soul. In Washington a group is meeting to prepare for the meeting with Frank. They are planning on using Frank's local hometown influence to gain the trust of the people in Prentice and open a door to stop this work. For some reason people in High places are concerned about the potential this place has.

CHAPTER TWELVE

THE IMPACT IS REVEALED

Time has passed and the months turned into years. Dustin is now 14 years old and there have been some challenges that threatened to stop Will's place. Last year Dustin was invited to visit the Whitehouse as a goodwill ambassador for special needs children. Word has gotten out that people from all over the world have been visiting the little town of Prentice and they are coming to see and listen to Dustin. The invitation was declined and an emissary from the Whitehouse was sent to find out why. His name is Wyatt and he traveled for three days to get here. He did not let anyone know who he was so he could get the facts without it being skewed. He arrived just as the group was gathering in the main hall. He stood outside by the big oak in the parking lot and watched as children of all nationalities pushed in wheel chairs or hobble their way to the two giant front doors. He thought of this whole thing as a scam for money and was really planning on exposing the whole thing. He had a strange feeling as he made his way to the front door and thought maybe this would be his chance to prove his worth. Walking on either side of him were two angels guarding his mind. They already banished the demon of manipulation and opened the door for the Lord to work on Wyatt's mind. He opened the door and was stopped in his tracks. His mind was racing and he suddenly found himself back in his childhood sitting on a hard old wooden church pew. He stared at the front of the building and saw a single lone figure standing and he was just looking up at the ceiling. Wyatt's mind took him back to an old country preacher talking about Jesus and giving his life to him. He remembered a time when he made a choice to repent and give his life to his faith. He listened to the young boy on the stage and was feeling as light as a feather. Without even knowing it he was walking down the aisle toward the stage. Without even knowing it he was kneeling at the front and crying like a little baby. When he looked up, Dustin was standing in front of him just looking down at him and smiling. "Mr. Wyatt, Father said he is glad you changed your mind. He remembered the promise you made him when you were a little boy and he has been waiting for you to come back." Wyatt was just staring and wondering what was happening. He spoke and couldn't understand why he was saying what he was saying, "Dustin, I was sent here to…" Dustin smiled at him and said, "Father knows you came to try and stop us. He even made a way for you to get here, but He has a better plan for you. He wants you to go back to the people that sent you and tell them God loves them. Father said don't be afraid. He will go in front of you and give you the words to speak." Wyatt got up and walked to his car and when he got in he just sat there and cried. How is he going to explain this, but at this point he didn't care?

The group from Washington has put everything in motion and is just waiting for Wyatt to get back with some important information. Powerful attorneys have created some legal roadblocks that will tie up the finances for Will's

Place and some powerful people with deep pockets have been able to prepare the way for several injunctions to halt the use of the property. Within a few days, federal agents will make their way to Will's Place and stop the activities. Tomorrow afternoon Wyatt will be back with the pictures and information necessary to set everything in motion, but little do they know the Lord has been working as well. Demons anxiously await the moment this will all fall into place. Strago is about to arrive and every demon of any worth is also waiting. Greed, hate, misery, fame, fortune, cheating, worry, deceit, lust, anger, paranoia, depression, and glory all pace back and forth. The old gentleman from the original meeting is sitting in a high back leather office chair drinking a little bourbon on the rocks and smoking a thick, foul smelling cigar. Just a few more hours and he will have revenge and everything that is due to him. He has such a hate for people of faith and how they manipulate. At least the way he manipulates is understandable and somewhat acceptable to the people he knows. Strago arrives and gathers all the forces together. The plan is working perfectly and this old man thinks he is in control, but he is nothing more than a toy being played with. Humans are such simple creatures and they don't realize how much is available to them. Strago remembers when Lucifer was able to mislead the first man and woman to doubt God and that was in a perfect setting with everything at their feet. This will be an enjoyable day because he knows the power of evil on the mind of mankind. Strago himself attacks the mind of this prideful, arrogant, self-praising human. People like him think they are so important and so smart, but little do they realize they are simply little pawns in a very large game that is playing for keeps.

Wyatt begins the drive back to Washington and as he drives he is rehearsing what he will say and do. Part of him wants to stand up and tell them what Dustin told him. If he totally commits his life to Jesus he can kiss his political future goodbye, Wyatt now has a partner that he doesn't even realize is on his side. The angel, Micah, has been waiting for Wyatt to come back to the Lord and now he will protect Wyatt as he accomplishes the will of the Father. As Wyatt drives he prays, "Father, I am so sorry that I didn't trust you all these years, but now I can see clearly who I am. I ask only for wisdom when I get back to Washington. Please, go before me and prepare me a table in front of my enemies." Wyatt has this new found energy that grabs his heart strings and makes him want to tell everyone what just took place. He is sure his friends will call him a fool and a traitor, but whatever happens. Wyatt will keep his eye on the prize and run the race with patience. Micah stays close by as Wyatt settles in for the long drive back and as he travels he is listening to gospel music and actually enjoying it.

The next morning at 9:45 the big conference room is filled with 15 people. 12 sit at the table and the other three are strategically seated in large leather chairs pushed up against the wall. At the head of the table is the elderly man who spoke to Frank years earlier and is now heading up this entire operation. In the corners of the room are dark aboding figures watching over this proceeding. Strago sits next to the old man and whispers in his ear. His disdain for this whole operation on the mountain has grown into an obsession. He not only hates the cause of Will's Place, but he sees amazing earning potential that could be turned into a huge profit making machine. Under the guise of helping others, this operation could be global if it is run correctly and the small town mentality has no concept of how to accomplish that. At that moment the door opens and Wyatt steps in. All chairs turn toward the door when they hear whistling, Wyatt smiles and waves. He has a briefcase in his hand and a new spring in his step. "Gooooood morning everyone. Isn't it a great day to be alive?" The old man looks at him with crossed brows and a scowl on his face then motions for him to sit down using a nod of his head. Wyatt takes a seat on the opposite end of the table, sets his briefcase down and un-latches the two gold locking mechanisms. He takes out a stack of papers and sets them on the table.

The old man opens the meeting by introducing Wyatt. "Gentlemen, I want to introduce my associate. He recently visited the operation I have been telling you about known as Will's Place. This is not only a threat to our beliefs, but it is potentially one of the largest money making operations I have seen in in life. The potential of this place is almost unlimited and can bring an estimated 15-20% return on any money you invest. With that being said, my associate has what we will need to finally take control of this place. Wyatt, the floor is yours." At that moment the Holy Spirit fills Wyatt with a boldness and assurance. As the demons surrounding the room sense the presence of God in the room they start frantically looking around. Strago commands them to go outside and keep an eye out for any warriors that might show up with instructions to delay them until this deal is done. They leave and make it outside just in time to see an amazing and frightful sight. Splitting the sky like a giant bolt of lightning is a stream of heavenly hosts. The fly straight at this place with amazing speed. The demons shriek in fear and make an attempt to stop this assault, but the angel in front is Micheal the Arch angel of Heaven. He bursts through the crowd of demons and goes directly into the board room. Strago sees him at the moment Micheal swings his sword. He strikes Strago across the chest and sends him reeling across the room and into the air on the outside of the building. As Strago gains his balance he is hit again. Micheal is relentless and as this battle ensues, the grace of God moves Wyatt inside the room.

Gentlemen, he is correct. Wyatt stands and continues "This is a powerful, well-funded, well backed operation. From my research there are people coming from around the globe and many of them have almost endless financial resources. In that group there are very powerful people with amazing political influence. The power this place yields is almost unprecedented." The old man smiles and looks around the room watching the approval of his associates. Wyatt shuffles some papers then continues. "I saw several dignitaries from several ally nations and even some from nations that are not so friendly to the United States. I saw a large group of disabled and needy children in wheel chairs or with what we might consider deformities. This in itself is enough to tug at people's hearts and make them open their hearts. It is estimated this is a one billion dollar a year business with potential for more and almost endless trusts set up in interest bearing accounts to produce even more." There is a growing excitement in the room as Wyatt continues, "This whole operation hinges on a 14 year old boy they call Dustin. He is mesmerizing and charismatic. He has the capability to know everything about you including your name. When he speaks it is like someone else is speaking and you can't control your emotions when you are watching and listening. You don't even realize he has Down Syndrome and a speech impediment. The old man leans over the table, smiles and says, "Well this is even better than I thought. A disabled child with charisma. Continue"

The demons influencing this group have been disbanded and in their place are angels, led by Micah, who now stands next to Wyatt. The group's demeanor has changed and their hearts are melting with the exception of the old man who has hardened his own heart to the place that it resembles that of Judas in the time of the Lord's time on earth. Betrayal is bound up in the heart and when a person makes that decision there is a hard outer seal on that heart that will not permit grace to enter. Wyatt clears his throat, smiles and says, "I have seen firsthand the power and potential of this place. Yes it is a money cow, but it is an amazingly powerful tool to change the world. When I walked into the main hall I saw hundreds of people looking toward a brightly lit stage and on that stage was a lone figure. I was like many of you and my skepticism caused me to watch with greed and dislike. But then something happened and I found my mind drifting to my childhood and a memory of an old country church and preacher. I recalled a choice I made when I was a child and before I knew it I was standing in front of this figure on the stage. His name is Dustin, and he is the 14 year old with Down Syndrome. He looked at me and smiled with a smile that was almost angelic." Everyone is on the edge of their seat listening intently. Wyatt continues, "He said to me, 'My Father said he is glad you came and has been waiting for you to return'. Gentlemen, I have returned. Not to this meeting to help you stop this movement, but returned to the God of my childhood when I made Jesus Christ the Lord of my life. I stand before you and speak the words of the apostles in that time after Jesus was resurrected and went back to heaven. Silver and gold have I none, but such as I have I give you. Jesus Christ is my Lord and Savior and I will not be instrumental in stopping this place, rather I will be its strongest ally and proponent. I advise any of you who decide to take on this endeavor to reconsider because you will be fighting against God himself and there is no chance you will win. The old man stands a slaps both hands on the table and screams, "that is enough. You have gone crazy and lost it. You are fired and will pay the consequences for betrayal." Wyatt looks at him and says with a smile, "I will not fear what man can do to me. Greater is he who is in me than he who is in the world." Heaven smiles while hell gathers forces.

Back at Will's place Skylar asks Jackson to meet her upstairs for a minute, she has something she needs to tell him before they go into the evening meeting. She sits on the bed with tears in her eyes. Jackson walks over to her and kneels besides her wondering what could possibly be wrong. Skylar takes his hand and places it on her stomach and smiles. Jackson looks up and her and his eyebrows rise as his smile grows. "Are you saying what I think you are saying"? Skylar smiles and says "yes, the Lord has also given me a name, His name is John."

The ministry has grown and Dustin has matured beyond what anyone thought he would or could. His DVD's are being sold around the world and the gospel message is being shared in regions where it was once denied entrance. Every night Dustin speaks and after every meeting he escapes to his prayer shed on the top of the mountain. This has taken its toll on his body, but no one knows that except Dustin. He is always happy and smiling in spite of the growing pain inside his body. On this particular night, he doesn't return at the usual time and after an hour of delay, Jackson walks up to the prayer shed. He peeks inside and sees Dustin laying on the floor. Kurios is standing watch as are other angels. Jackson opens the door and see's Dustin just lying there with his eyes open but he is not moving. Panic and fear grip Jackson's heart and mind He lifts Dustin in his arms and begins the walk to the main house. Heaven is not surprised and the Fathers palm is right on schedule.

THE END

Printed in the United States
By Bookmasters